MURIEL JENSEN

MAKE-BELIEVE MOM

Harlequin Books

TORONTO • NEW YORK • LONDON
AMSTERDAM • PARIS • SYDNEY • HAMBURG
STOCKHOLM • ATHENS • TOKYO • MILAN
MADRID • WARSAW • BUDAPEST • AUCKLAND

ISBN 0-373-16534-X

MAKE-BELIEVE MOM

Copyright © 1994 by Muriel Jensen.

This edition published by arrangement with Harlequin Enterprises B. V.

® and TM are trademarks of the publisher. Trademarks indicated with
® are registered in the United States Patent and Trademark Office, the
Canadian Trade Marks Office and in other countries.

Printed in U.S.A.

Chapter One

Barbara Ryan studied the can of garbanzo beans on her desk and waited for inspiration to strike. Nothing happened.

She rolled her chair backward to the wall of her small cubicle in search of a different perspective. There had to be one. Successful advertising worked on one of two basic principles—creating an image for the product, or motivating the consumer to action.

Two hours ago she'd tried to imagine mobilizing consumers into an army on the march for garbanzos, but she'd decided to attempt to give the bean charm and appeal instead—to create the image. The entire staff of Cheney & Roman had gone to lunch, and she was still sitting there, staring at the twelve-ounce can.

She tilted her head and wiggled the pencil caught between her fingers, trying to relax and encourage thought to flow. But the sounds of construction from the opposite side of the office challenged her ability to concentrate.

Barbara put on the ear protectors that had been provided by the management when work had begun a week ago and tried to concentrate on what she'd learned about garbanzos. They were also called chick-peas. Chick-peas. She had an instant mental image of a cuddly chick-pea emerging from an egg and weaving around on little chick feet.

She groaned, mentally erased the thought and tried again. Nutlike flavor, good in minestrone and Spanish stew. A garbanzo with castanets!

Get real, Ryan, she told herself firmly. Garbanzos could get her out of the copywriting bleachers and into the game. She could get one of the more stylish accounts, gain some attention, take a step up the rickety corporate ladder. *Think!*

The health aspect of beans was important. And healthy eating had snob appeal for young and old alike. Maybe that was it—a doctor in pristine whites, his stethoscope around his neck, standing in the rice and beans aisle of the grocery store, extolling the virtues of the bulbous little bean.

The muted but still audible sounds of hammering and ripping provided a very appropriate background for such an awful idea.

"Barb, here's the dress!"

Carol McDonald stood breathlessly in the doorway of Barbara's cubicle and held up a long plastic dress sleeve with the name of a chic boutique emblazoned on it. Underneath was a silky dark blue dress that shimmered even in the dim light of her tiny office.

Barbara gasped as she reached across the small space and lifted the plastic wrapper. Tiny beads sparkled like the night sky.

"Are you sure you want to lend this to me?" she asked, as Carol perched on the end of her desk. "I'll be wearing it to a dinner, and I'd die if anything happened to it."

Carol was a tall redhead whose desk in front of the boss's office was covered with photos of her two-year-old. She waved a careless hand. "I haven't worn it since I got pregnant with Casey. I hate to leave her at night when I've been gone all day, so Jerry has to entertain his clients without me. But you have a man to impress. Try it on."

"Good idea." Barbara indicated her doorless office and the racket coming from the ladies' room, where the crew was ripping up old plumbing. "Where do you suggest I do that?"

"In Mr. Cheney's office." Carol tugged Barbara out of her chair and turned her bodily in that direction.

Barbara resisted as Carol pushed. "I can't do that. His office is locked and I . . ."

"Of course you can. He's out of town until tomorrow afternoon. The office is empty, he has a floor-to-ceiling mirror in his private bathroom, and you happen to be on personal terms with his secretary." She batted long eyelashes dramatically as she pointed to herself with a graceful index finger. "Come on. I'll let you in."

"Carol—"

"Ryan, tonight you're going to meet the man and woman who gave birth to the man you're dating. Why you're dating him is a mystery to me, but that's your business." Carol ignored the roll of Barbara's eyes and went on. "Trevor is handsome, he's successful and he's . . . sort of . . ."

"Intelligent and kind," Barbara put in as Carol groped for words.

Carol retrieved a key from the middle drawer of her desk and grinned at Barbara. "I was going to say stuffy."

Barbara nudged Carol in the backside with her knee as her friend unlocked the door. "He's not stuffy. He just takes his work very seriously."

"Barb, he gave you an *IRA* for your birthday. He even thinks of *you* in terms of money. I think you should throw him back." Carol pulled her inside and closed the door.

"He is not a fish, Carol. He's a man. And he's entitled to his eccentricities. Given his work, he probably thought an IRA was a very special gift."

Carol eyed her steadily. "You were disappointed."

"I was . . . surprised."

John Cheney's office was large—but functional, rather than elegant. Neat piles of mail, faxes and telephone messages sat atop the desk along with the usual pencil cup, an assortment of framed photos, a call director and a calendar.

The chair was high-backed brown leather, and a small matching sofa sat under a window that looked out onto the port of Portland. The office was quiet as a tomb.

Carol opened a door that led into a spacious bathroom complete with the full-length mirror she had promised.

Barbara stood on the threshold and peered into the bathroom. It was done in black and white and had a tub, a Jacuzzi, a shower and a sauna.

John Cheney did seem like the kind of man who expected his conveniences. Barbara had never spoken to him, except on her first day six months ago when Carol had taken her on a tour of the office and introduced her to the partners.

Hal Roman was short and a little paunchy and always smiling from ear to ear.

By contrast Cheney was tall, dark and gorgeous. She remembered that he'd stood to lean across his desk and shake her hand, and she'd felt his energy and the impact of his gaze. All the women in the office whispered about his good looks, but she found them almost too wolfish for comfort.

He had the honey-colored eyes of a wolf, a strong, straight nose and a smile as ready as his partner's—except that his was more feral.

She'd been happy to learn that Hal Roman oversaw the employees, while John Cheney dealt with clients.

"I'm starved," Carol said, handing her the dress. "Shall I run down to Rubio's and bring back soft-shell tacos while you're changing?"

Barbara hugged her with her free arm. "Please. And thanks for taking most of your lunch hour to go home to get the dress."

Carol dismissed Barb's gratitude with a wave of her hand.

"That's what friends are for—to come through for you when the cleaners ruins your favorite frock."

Barbara closed the door behind Carol, hung the dress on a hook on the door and pushed off her black flats. She unpinned the loose knot of her hair, then pulled the teal and fuchsia sweater over her head.

Seeing her reflection in the mirror, she laughed. She looked like a warning against using the wrong shampoo.

She slipped out of her slacks, folded everything on the closed commode, then pulled the plastic sleeve from Carol's dress. In the bright fluorescent light of the bathroom it glittered like an angel's garb.

Barbara stepped back and simply admired it. It would be snug, she guessed, and would reveal a little bosom. She felt a thrill of excitement.

She was taking a step toward the dress, arms raised to reach for the hanger, when the door burst open.

JOHN CHENEY dropped his briefcase and jacket on his desk, pulled at his tie and headed for the shower. As he pushed his way into the bathroom, his mind was filled with all the details he had to put together for his upcoming impromptu appointment.

A startled little scream stopped him in his tracks. He was completely shocked to find himself with a fragrant, half-naked young woman in his arms. He stared into dark brown eyes and at a stream of dark hair and was about to decide he could happily adjust to the situation when she leapt backward.

She collided with the towel rack, and a thick black bath sheet slithered to the floor.

"Oh, no," she said, rubbing her shoulder with one hand while reaching for the towel with the other—keeping her eyes on him all the time as though she expected him to pounce. "Mr. Cheney, I'm so sorry!"

Even before she used his name he realized she worked for him. He guessed it was the way she was dressed—or *un*dressed—that had confused him.

This was Ryan from Domestic Products. The young woman who'd saved Barnett's hide with the charter boat slogan. Usually all he saw of her was the dark coil of hair at the back of her head and the square, slender shoulders facing her computer terminal.

He'd had no idea what he'd been missing.

Those ivory shoulders were anything but stiff in the cap sleeves of a low-cut black silk teddy. Her small high breasts appeared above the towel she clutched as she took a startled breath. She had straight hips and the thighs of a young man's dreams. They emerged from the high French cut of the teddy, leading his eyes down to shapely knees and long calves that ended in a trim ankle and the incongruous note of teal blue socks.

Barbara's breath caught in her throat. Surprise, embarrassment and the warm sensation of John Cheney's hands on her bare arms combined to stall her brain.

She tried to think. She didn't intend to lie about how she'd gotten in here, but she had to cover for Carol. And now that her employer had gotten over the initial shock of finding a woman in his bathroom, a suspicious frown was forming between his golden eyes.

He appeared even taller without the pulled-together look a jacket gave a man, and the stark whiteness of his shirt against his tanned face and hands was dramatic.

She watched one of those hands now as he reached behind himself for the door handle, to close and lock the door. Her heartbeat accelerated.

John had to push away the thought that her white skin and black silk outfit made her look as though she'd been designed to be placed just where she stood—just for him—and made himself think about what her presence here could mean. New-Age Advertising had underbid them on several new accounts in the past few months and he and Hal were getting suspicious. The bids and the proposal were so close that they would have to have had inside information on the Cheney & Roman plans.

"Let's determine why you're in here," he said, folding his arms, "before we decide whether either one of us is sorry about it."

Barbara blinked, not entirely sure what he was suggesting. Did he think she'd lain in wait for him in her underwear?

She dropped one hand from the towel and pointed to the dress hanging behind him on the door.

"Carol is lending me that dress for a party tonight," she explained with a swallow. "I was trying it on."

"This office was locked," he said sternly.

"Yes, but you were supposed to be away until tomorrow," she stated reasonably. "And the bathrooms aren't usable for a few days. I apologize. I used poor judgment."

"You must have also used a key," he said implacably. "The door hasn't been tampered with."

That was safe enough to admit. "Yes, I did."

"And where did you get it?"

"From Carol's desk."

"She keeps it locked."

"She'd stepped away for coffee. Mr. Cheney . . ."

He put his hands in his pockets and asked quietly, "What did you expect to find in my office?"

"A mirror!" she replied a little loudly, patience thinning. "Do I look as though I'm dressed for industrial espionage?"

He wasn't sure what to think. Carol usually guarded the privacy of his office as though she were armed. On the other hand, Barbara Ryan's dark eyes reflected embarrassment and impatience, but not guilt.

"I'm sure," he said, fixing her with those wolf's eyes, "that espionage of all kinds is often conducted just this way. A man comes home to find a beautiful woman among his things, and she makes him forget to wonder what she's doing there."

Barbara, unsettled by the notion that she was capable of disorienting him, dropped the towel long enough to pick up her pile of clothes and cover as much of herself as she could. It wasn't much.

"But you didn't forget to wonder, did you?" She gave him a cool, affronted tilt of her chin. "First you suggested I was here to somehow ensnare you, and then you as much as accused me of looking through your office."

"Did you?"

"No! Now, if I'm fired, I'll leave. If I'm not, I'd appreciate it if you'd let me pass so I can get back to work."

"Without trying on the dress?"

She groaned. The dress. She'd almost forgotten the damn thing.

He relented, convinced she was innocent of everything but wanting to use his bathroom. He would have to speak to Carol about keeping a closer eye on her keys. Or maybe he wouldn't. This had certainly brightened a dull, working weekend.

"Very well." He stepped aside and opened the door. "But I'd have liked to see you in it."

Barbara sailed forward, eyes averted. He caught her arm, his grinning glance running the length of her. "Maybe you'd better put something on before you go out there."

She pulled away from him, then stopped in the middle of his office and backed away from him toward the door. "Everyone's at lunch," she said, anxious to get away. "I'll dress in my cubicle."

Then without warning the office door burst open, and a man with a wide smile walked in, saying in a booming but cheerful voice, "Hey, John. I know we're early but I have to handle hospital rounds for... ah... oh!"

The man stopped short, his hand still on the doorknob, when he caught sight of Barbara's skimpy attire. Another man coming in behind him collided with his back, and they were pushed four steps farther into the office as the four people behind *him* slapped into each other like dominoes.

Five figures fanned out around the first man to see what had stopped him. In her embarrassment, Barbara noticed only two details. One of the group was a woman. And they were all wearing clerical collars.

She didn't even wonder what the clergy was doing here, or why they'd descended on her en masse. She just knew this day was developing into something that made garbanzo beans seem as usual as white bread. She considered doing herself in with an airbrush or by drinking the art department's coffee.

Everyone stood in silence. Barbara could imagine how lewd this must appear to the men and woman of the cloth. She opened her mouth to explain, hoping something would come out.

John found himself more amused than horrified. Ryan was clutching her clothes to her, her cheeks pink, her eyes closed. He imagined she struggled over forming an explanation.

He, on the other hand, rarely found it necessary to explain himself. But this was a touchy situation. Cheney & Roman had a lot to lose if Daniel Burger and his group misunderstood this interesting tableau.

As Ryan opened her mouth, apparently ready with the explanation, he took action. He walked past her to the man who'd led the assault on his office.

"Daniel!" Barbara watched her employer shake the first man's hand with every appearance of hospitality. "Welcome to Cheney & Roman."

Daniel looked doubtfully from Barbara to his host. "Hello, John. I'm...sorry. I had a scheduling change this morning and, since you were fitting us in on a day when you aren't supposed to be here, anyway, I thought you might not mind if we arrived fifteen minutes early." He looked guiltily at Barbara. "It seems that wasn't a good idea."

Cheney laughed lightly. "Well, you did catch us a little off guard."

Barbara, still clutching her pile of clothes to her, felt a stab of alarm when he turned to her with a smile and extended his hand. Taking it would have meant freeing the shoes that she held atop the pile. Instead, she went hesitantly toward him, sure he was about to explain to his guests how she'd broken into his office, taken over his bathroom and caused this embarrassing little debacle.

That wasn't what he did.

It wasn't even close.

John Cheney wrapped an arm around her shoulders and pulled her to his side. Then he inclined his head and kissed her—briefly, quickly, but with the ease of a man who had the right. She was too surprised to object.

"Gentlemen," he said, "Mrs. Gordon, may I present my wife, Barbara. Darling, this is..." He went down a list of names and church affiliations, but she didn't hear a thing. She was too busy smiling and trying not to undermine his deception by letting her mouth fall open.

By the time he finished introductions, she could see the cleverness of his ploy. Of course. His wife. She had to applaud his quick thinking. Certainly even the clergy couldn't condemn a man's lust for his own wife in his own office.

"We've only been married a short time," he said, apparently trying to give the fiction substance.

Barbara accepted that she'd gotten him into this and owed him a good performance. She looked up at him with a reverence she was sure they'd understand. And she took a little satisfaction in the fact that he seemed surprised by her cooperation. "And he's been away for several days. He got back just before you arrived, and I'm afraid I tried to distract him from business."

The man he'd called Daniel fixed her with a confused smile. "But we met him at the CC breakfast this morning."

"CC?" she asked in a small voice, wishing she hadn't decided to be heroic.

"Daniel and his group," Cheney explained, looking pleased that her effusion had almost thwarted her, "are the board of directors for the Cooperative Churches. I came back from Denver a day early to attend their breakfast and get a feel for what they're looking for in their ad campaign. You remember. I explained when I called you last night."

"Oh, yes," she said a little too brightly. "Right!"

"Our discussion this morning went so well that I suggested we meet here after lunch so I can show them exactly what we can do for them."

She nodded and saw her opportunity to recapture her role. "So my plan to meet you here and charm you into coming home early was a bad idea."

John was intrigued to see that she was good at this, fast on her feet. And despite the urgency of the moment, he couldn't help but stop and consider what they'd be doing right now if that look in her eye were genuine and she *had* intended to charm him. Then he had to let the thought go. The distraction was too great—and too dangerous.

A gleam in his eye told her that her rejoinder had been a good move. He kissed her temple. She noted abstractedly that his lips were warm and dry. "It was a great idea," he said in a low, suggestive tone. "Just one we'll have to pursue later. Maybe you'd better get dressed."

She smiled apologetically at the group, which now looked at her indulgently rather than critically. "I've enjoyed meeting you," she lied. "I'll just slip out when I leave." She smiled up at Cheney, thinking something more might be required in front of their audience. "I'll see you at home," she said softly.

She saw the challenge in his eyes, felt the slightest pressure of the hand that now held her elbow. She tipped her face up. He intercepted her lips with his, gave her one heartfelt kiss that completely upset her equilibrium, then walked her to the bathroom, pushed her gently inside and closed the door.

Barbara locked herself in and fell against the door, gasping for air and praying for her emotional and physical balance to be restored. She was going to kill Carol.

She knew she was flirting with fate, but she took an extra moment to slip on the blue dress. She stood on tiptoe to create the impression of wearing heels and turned to study her reflection—and remind herself what had started all this in the first place.

She was going to meet Trevor's parents. The very thought calmed her. Trevor was potential husband material—steady, reliable, calm. So Carol insisted he was stodgy. That wasn't a bad trait. Barbara's father had been a flamboyant architect with all the excitement in his life anyone could want—and none of the stability. He'd always been somewhere across the globe or deep in a creative frenzy whenever she needed him. He was now working on a shopping complex in Tokyo, and her mother had married a doctor.

The dress was beautiful, and what was even more important, it made *her* beautiful. It clung everywhere, the long column of shimmering silk dramatizing her height and highlighting her slenderness. The low, draped neckline suggested but did not display cleavage.

This wasn't the style of dress one would normally wear to meet a man's parents, but Trevor would be receiving an award at a formal dinner and they were flying in from Palm Beach.

She studied the low neckline in concern for a moment, wondering what his parents would think. Then she laughed softly as she quickly but carefully pulled the dress off. Even if they disapproved, their thoughts would probably be mild compared to those of the clergy on the other side of the door.

Barbara groaned aloud as she hung the dress again and pulled on her clothes. If her cheeks weren't still hot pink, she'd be wondering if that whole fiasco had ever happened.

Of course, that was the story of her life—good intentions that went awry, innocent adventures that had a way of turning on her. Well, she'd escaped this one unscathed, and she was grateful to be getting out with her skin—even though everyone had seen it.

Her mother insisted it was because she was like her father that trouble always found her. She wanted so much to prove that wasn't true.

It was time to get serious. She loved her job, and she fully intended to one day be invaluable to Cheney & Roman. But she wanted a home and children, too. She wanted life insurance and a station wagon to drive the kids to ballet and tuba lessons. She wanted to buy in family-size quantities and learn to use leftovers.

She brushed her hair, freshened her makeup, tossed the dress over her arm and squared her shoulders. "All right," she told herself aloud. "They're going to be deep in a marketing discussion. Keep your eyes front and your pace quick, and you're out of here."

She had so convinced herself a hasty retreat was possible that when she opened the door to find everyone in the office staring at her, it stopped her cold. Every occupant of the six chairs pulled in a semicircle around Cheney's desk studied her with eerily intense concentration.

Her "husband" sat on the corner of his desk, his jacket tossed back on his chair, his tie pulled away from his throat. She saw a kind of amused resignation in his eyes and felt her heart sink to her stomach. She didn't know what that look meant, and she was sure she didn't want to know.

"Well." She smiled brightly, carefully avoiding her employer's eyes as she backed across the office. "Have a lovely afternoon, everyone. I have places to go and people to see."

She sailed as far as the door, under the steam of determination. Then John Cheney said her name.

"Barbara."

It was nothing, just her name. But she'd been Barb since childhood. Friends called her Barb. Trevor called her Barb.

The rolling syllables of her full name rode off Cheney's tongue like some mystical spell—as though he'd called to something inside her attuned to the lyrical sound. She turned.

He smiled and beckoned. "Can you stay a minute? Daniel has an idea he'd like to run by you."

She didn't like the sound of that at all. She had no idea why; she just didn't. But seven pairs of eyes were staring at her, and John Cheney's were trying to tell her something.

Intrepidly, because she felt she owed it to him to play her "wifely" role until these people finally left, she hung the dress hanger on the hat rack by the door and went to the edge of desk he'd cleared for her beside him.

The moment she was seated, Daniel Burger rested an elbow on the arm of his chair and leaned toward her. "My colleagues and I," he said with that ever-present smile, "want to launch an advertising campaign that will bring young people back to the church."

She nodded, trying to sound knowledgeable without encouraging what he had in mind—at least until she knew what it was. "I believe that's already a trend, isn't it?"

He bobbed his head from side to side in a gesture that was indeterminate. "If it is, it isn't moving fast enough for us. Attendance is way down in most churches." Everyone nodded.

Barbara felt Cheney's arm come around her to settle carelessly across her shoulders. She got the impression it was intended to hold her in place. She braced herself.

"Your husband likes our plan," Daniel said. "And we hope you will, too."

"But I have no say in campaign devel—"

"You would in this one."

She refused to ask the logical question, afraid of the answer. He gave it to her, anyway.

"Because we want to find a couple that typifies the young American family, to show them in all their worldly pursuits, in their home, with their children, at their leisure—" His voice quieted. "In their obvious delight in each other."

She began to see it coming and decided Cheney had known what he was doing when he'd put his arm

around her. Given the opportunity to bolt, she would
be in Kansas by nightfall.

Daniel's voice regained its firm tenor as he went on.
"And show them at worship so everyone can see that
a man and woman in tune with the world they live in
still have room for God in their lives." He smiled be-
atifically. "We think you two would be perfect!"

Chapter Two

A portly man with thick white hair leaned forward. "John and the twins have been coming to St. Bonaventure's since I arrived two months ago." He gave her a questioning smile. "But I haven't seen you with them, Mrs. Cheney."

Her brain crowded by panic, Barbara tried desperately to think. Admitting that she didn't go to church would probably get her out of this dangerous situation, but it would also scotch the deal for Cheney & Roman.

"I've been spending weekends with my mother," she said. The lie came out smoothly, despite the turbulence inside her. "She hasn't been very well."

The priest frowned in concern. "Perhaps I should call on her."

"She's beginning to improve," Barbara said quickly, brightly, wondering what her very healthy Methodist mother would do if a Catholic priest appeared at her door, offering to comfort her in her illness. "She's able to get around now."

The priest nodded. "Well, the offer stands."

"Thank you, Father."

"Will you do it, Barbara?" Daniel asked. "John thinks all our ideas can be incorporated into the campaign, and we're excited at the prospect. We'd intended to simply hire models—until we saw the two of you together. You're a handsome couple and very much in love. That'll shine through with complete honesty."

The only woman among them shook her head. She had short, fair hair and, Barbara had noticed, a perpetual frown. "I have to object once again. I think we'd be safer with models." She cast a swift glance at Barbara that registered disapproval. "Granted, they seem very much in love, but if they quarrel, that will also come through with complete honesty."

"That's not a problem, Joanna," Daniel said. "Lovers can quarrel and still care deeply for each other. Disagreement is healthy. People understand that."

Joanna sat back quietly without further comment.

"Of course, we don't want you to feel coerced into agreeing to do this," Daniel said. "It'll mean someone from your staff and one of our representatives, living with you, photographing you, observing you, for the next few weeks. You should know that."

John turned slightly to flip the pages of his calendar on the desk behind him. "We have a conflict at the end of next week. It's my parents' anniversary, and we'll be spending a few days there."

Father O'Neil slapped Daniel on the shoulder. "That would be perfect. Three generations celebrating together, showing how we can live our own lives and still be drawn back to the family that nurtured us." He beamed at Barbara. "One of our most important messages is that love once given can be carried down the generations."

Barbara was truly beginning to feel like a fraud. What had begun as a harmless and very temporary deception was assuming potentially lethal proportions. She had to do something.

John had little trouble seeing the tension in her smile.

"Can we talk about this before we decide?" she asked.

He squeezed her shoulders, applying as much pressure as reassurance. "Of course. Daniel, I'll call you in the morning with our decision. If this doesn't work, I'll have an alternate plan in place in time for you to start this project at the end of the week, anyway. Meanwhile, my partner will show you some of our previous campaigns so you'll be able to see firsthand what we can do for you."

John picked up his telephone and asked Hal Roman to show the group around. He appeared instantly; the short, round embodiment of good cheer. Shaking hands with the group, he did a double take at the sight of John with an arm around a copywriter he knew his partner seldom saw.

"Daniel," John said to Hal, "wants to use Barbara and me as the models for their campaign."

Hal raised an eyebrow. "You and . . . Barbara?"

John nodded. "Barbara's a little reluctant." He squeezed her to him in a show of husbandly tolerance. "We're still jealous of our privacy. Nauseating newlyweds, you know."

"Newlyweds," Hal said slowly.

John replied with the slightest emphasis, "Right."

Barbara knew that word around the office was that John Cheney and Hal Roman were so successful because they read each other's minds and, creatively at least, they were in perfect sync.

Hal nodded a little vaguely, treading carefully. "When you called me about this after your breakfast meeting, you said to round up some models."

Daniel beamed. "Then we arrived a little early and walked in on John and Barbara...and saw how much in love they are, and got the idea to use them instead."

Hal looked blank and a little desperate.

"We'll talk it all over later," John said briskly. "Right now I'd appreciate it if you'd show them some of our past print and broadcast campaigns before they leave."

"Ah...right, sure."

Daniel stood and the rest of his group followed. He shook hands with John, then Barbara.

That close to him, her hand locked in his large, firm one, Barbara saw wisdom, strength, compassion and determination in the minister. She wondered if he saw the truth in her.

"All I ask," he said quietly, as John saw everyone else to the door, "is that you understand that we don't want to invade your privacy, we just want to show people what you have and convince them that they can have it, too. And that we know Who can help them find it." He placed his other hand atop their joined ones and pressed. "Goodbye."

When the door closed behind the Cooperative Churches members, Barbara faced John Cheney in the middle of his tobacco brown carpet.

He guessed by her mutinous expression that she was about to refuse to cooperate. He couldn't let that happen. He wanted very much to keep Daniel Burger and his group happy, and he wasn't averse to doing something good for himself at the same time. And Ryan was the most interesting woman to cross his path in a long while. The prospect of several weeks spent in intimate circumstances with her certainly brightened his horizon.

"I won't do this," she said, as he walked slowly toward her. "It would never work. And I'm practically engaged."

He caught her arm and pulled her gently with him toward the leather sofa before the window. "How can you be 'practically' engaged? Either you are or you aren't."

She placed a knee on the sofa and sat facing him, an elbow on the back. She kept her expression firm. "I've been seeing someone for almost a year. I couldn't possibly pre—"

John sat in the same position, the knee of his pin-striped pants just an inch from her woolen slacks, careful not to touch her. "Has he asked you to be his wife?"

"Not yet, but his parents are—"

"Then, you're not engaged."

She expelled an impatient puff of air. "All right, if you want to be technical, my feelings are engaged, even if my person isn't. I cannot pretend to be your wife for this ad campaign. Trevor is . . ."

"Trevor?" He raised an eyebrow and bit back a smile. "Very dramatic name. Was that dress intended to push him over the edge into matrimony?"

"No," she said tightly, obviously irritated.

John could see she didn't like to be teased.

"No," she said more quietly. "It was intended to replace my dress that was ruined by the cleaners. I hadn't time or money to buy one suitable, so Carol..."

"Suitable to what?"

"Suitable to the awards dinner being held in Trevor's honor this evening at the Downtown Hyatt. So Carol is lending me her dress."

He nodded dryly. "Right. Carol. Incidentally, she explained to me how you got into the office. It was noble of you to take the blame." While Barbara had been in the washroom, he'd made a quick trip to Carol's desk to ask her to bring coffee for his guests, and she'd explained everything. It touched him that Barbara had tried to protect her.

"Well..." She imitated that dismissing wave of Carol's. "I know she shouldn't have done it, and I didn't want you to fire her or anything."

He shook his head, negating that possibility. "I couldn't function without Carol. But I'd have thought someone so concerned about a friend would extend that concern to the problems caused by her unauthorized use of my office."

"I was in your bathroom," she reminded him quietly, "not your office."

"In your underwear." He used the same controlled tone. "In which my potential client saw you and would have assumed the worst had I not intervened."

"I was about to explain," she said defensively. "It would have absolved you of blame and cleared up the entire misunderstanding."

He smiled, thinking he had her. "Do you think for a moment they'd have believed you were in my office to try on a dress? Mrs. Gordon, particularly?"

Barbara opened her mouth to assure him that they would have, then closed it, knowing they wouldn't. The scene had been just too incriminating.

"Since you don't seem to have a conscience," he said, "I have to insist that you pretend to be my wife for this campaign."

"Mr. Cheney, I know nothing about you," she protested in desperation. "I mean, I've heard Carol talk about your kids, but I don't even know if you're widowed, divorced—"

"I'm neither," he replied. "I guess I'm what you'd call an unwed father." His smile was ironic. "I lived with a woman who became pregnant with my child. Well, we thought it was a single child at the time. She didn't want it, but I did, so I took care of the expenses, then took the babies."

Barbara was completely surprised. She was sure that situation happened rarely. Even men who were willing to take financial responsibility for an out-of-wedlock child were usually eager to have the woman, or some adoption agency, assume personal responsibility. She shook off a mental image of little wolf cubs.

"Daniel said we'd be studied and photographed for two weeks. I'd have to... to..."

"Move in with me," he provided, his gold eyes steady as he watched for her reaction. "Eat with me, sleep with me."

"That's out of the question."

"I'm afraid it's the only answer."

She folded her arms stubbornly. "I accept that this is all my fault, but, much as I love my job, I'm not willing to climb into your bed to save the company."

He nodded affably. "That's fine, as long as you convince the CC representative, and the camera, that you've done it."

"I don't think a woman can fake the wifely glow."

The telephone rang and he ignored it. His smile was wicked and slow. "Let me take you close enough that you'll imagine what it would be like. That might be enough to fool them."

She stared at him a moment, as though trying to decide whether or not he was serious.

He pressed. "The Cooperative Churches promises to be a lucrative account for us. If the Northwest campaign works, they intend to present it to their national board. And you can't dismiss the worthiness of the issue. This account would give us national prestige."

"Then, let them do it with models."

"They want us."

"But, we're a *lie*. You don't think the camera will pick that up?"

"No. We're simply an untried element." He smiled, the dangerous gold eyes going over her, then settling on her mouth. "Had I gotten to know you before this forced us together, I'd have made a point of knowing you better, and by this time you wouldn't have to fake anything with me. Anything at all."

Her balance tottered dangerously again. She fought to hold on to it. "I don't *think* so. I'm engaged, remember?"

He shook his head. "He hasn't asked you, remember?"

The buzzer sounded on his call director. He pushed himself off the sofa and leaned over the desk.

"Yes, Carol?" he asked into the speaker.

Carol's voice, sounding subdued, replied, "It's your daughter, Mr. Cheney."

"Thank you." He pushed the blinking light and picked up the reciever. "Hi, baby. What is it?"

Barbara stood to leave, but he put a hand out in a halting gesture. Frustrated, she wandered around the office while he talked.

"Yes, I missed you, too. How've you guys been?" He listened for a moment, then Barbara saw him put a hand to his eyes and shake his head. "No. No. Jade, you weigh less than seventy pounds. You can't have an ATV. No, Joe isn't getting one, no matter what he told you." He shook his head at Barbara as he sat on the edge of his desk. "Yeah, I know. Well, I'd move to Jurassic Park with the other dinosaurs if it really existed. Ask Libby if she needs anything from the store on my way home." He waited a moment. "All right. I'll be there in about an hour. Love you, too. Yeah, sure. Put him on."

John made a helpless gesture with one hand, then returned his attention to the phone.

"Hi, Joe. Yeah. No, well, you know how women are. You have to be specific."

He grinned at Barbara when she sent him a cool look.

"Well, next time explain that it's a plan and not a reality. I'm not sure you could ride an ATV all the way to Boston, anyway. All-terrain vehicles are only off-road, you know, and you might have a problem when you get to the Rockies. Well, get a map out and we'll plan it after dinner. Right. Love you, too. Bye."

John hung up the phone, still smiling. Barbara could see that the feelings that prompted the smile also lit his eyes and lent him a tenderness she hadn't seen before. She found herself speculating on the private life of the paradoxical John Cheney. For an instant she even entertained the notion of becoming a part of it, if only temporarily. Then she shook off the thought, remembering how easily she got into trouble.

"That remark about knowing women sounded to me as though you're raising a little chauvinist," she scolded gently.

He nodded with a laugh. "He does have tendencies that way, but his sister thinks of herself as a cross between George Custer and General Patton, so they'll cancel each other out when they grow up."

He sobered, she squared her shoulders, and they studied each other in silence for a moment. Then she asked without preamble, "What if I refuse to play the part of your wife?"

"Then," he said with a reluctant sigh, "I guess I'll have to stop playing the part of your employer." He didn't want this opportunity—personal as well as professional—to slip away.

Barbara required several seconds to understand what he meant. Then she examined his studiedly innocent expression and asked pointedly, "You mean you'd fire me?"

"I mean," he replied, his wolf's eyes not quite carrying off the ingenuous gaze, "I'd have to conclude you don't have the interests of Cheney & Roman at heart."

She refused to give him the satisfaction of her indignation. "That's harassment."

He did not appear intimidated. "Of an employee whom I found inside my locked office in my absence."

Now she didn't care who saw her indignation. "I explained that! I took nothing and damaged nothing!"

"You were in your underwear, Barbara."

She doubled her fists in frustration. "Fine! Then you're free to take me to court, and *you* can explain to the CC why you lied to them about my being your wife. *I* was going to tell the truth!"

He shook his head with that same expression of regret. "Then I'd lose a client and you'd lose your job, probably your reputation and very likely the proposal you seem to feel so sure is in your future. If I were you, I'd give it all a second thought."

"My answer," she said firmly, "is no! Would you like me to clear out my desk?"

"I'd like you to think about it overnight."

"I don't have to."

"Good. I'll call Daniel in the morning and tell him you've agreed."

"But I said—"

He opened his door and was pushing her gently through. He peered around the corner to speak to Carol. "Get Morgenthaler on the phone for me, please. And get me a double cap."

"Right." Carol picked up the phone.

"Mr. Cheney..." Barbara caught his shirtsleeve, trying to stop him as he stepped back into his office.

He looked down at her fingers clutching his shirtsleeve, then into her eyes. She freed him immediately.

"Morgenthaler on the phone," Carol said.

He grinned. "I rather like the idea of you clutching at me. Excuse me. I have a call." And he closed the door.

Barbara turned to Carol with fire in her eyes, but her friend cradled the phone on her shoulder and made a cross of her fingers to hold her away.

"Hi," she said into the receiver while smiling at Barbara. "This is Carol at Cheney & Roman. I need a double cappuccino for Mr. Cheney. Chocolate on the top. Right. Thanks."

As she hung up the telephone, she handed Barbara a paper bag. "Your taco," she said. "Eat, you'll feel better. I know, I know..." She raised a restraining hand as Barbara prepared to tell her what letting her into Cheney's office had caused. "He told me briefly what happened, when he stepped out to ask me to get the CC's coffee. I'm sorry I insisted you use his bathroom, but look at how it turned out."

Carol was beaming, Barbara noted, as though what had happened had been somehow positive.

"I'm *not* going to do it. Trevor wouldn't like it, I couldn't possibly pull it off, and someone would surely find out and we'd all be in worse trouble. It's an absurd idea."

Carol sobered. "Barbara. You're responsible for his predicament."

Barbara narrowed her eyes. "*Who's* responsible?"

Carol stood to follow her as she stalked back to her cubicle. Carol stood in the doorway and leaned a shoulder against the opening.

"He and Mr. Roman have worked so hard for this contract," she said gravely. "But the CC was having difficulty getting everyone to agree. When they called while Mr. Cheney was gone, I told them how to reach him in Denver. Unfortunately, he made the plans to come back a day early and neglected to tell me. I guess inviting them back here was all very impromptu."

Barbara delved into her paper bag, took a sniff of cold taco and tossed the bag and its contents away. "Very unfortunate for all of us. But I can't help it. If anyone should pretend to be his wife, it should be you."

Carol came to lean against the lineup of print ads Barbara had tacked up on her corkboard wall. "We need this account, Barb. Cheney & Roman's reputation for integrity and excellence has earned them more local work than we can manage, but they need national exposure. If this account works locally, they'll go national with it."

"He explained that to me."

"Then how can you say no?"

"Because it would take two weeks. *Two weeks* of living with him in intimate circumstances, being with his children, pretending to know things about him I don't know, being photographed..."

Carol nodded calmly. "His kids are great, he lives in a Georgian mansion in the woods that has every convenience a woman could want, and he's not all that complicated."

Barbara sighed, feeling control slip away from her. "All men are complicated."

Carol shook her head. "Men who think of everything in terms of money are complicated, maybe because the dollar goes up and down, and the exchange rate is always changing. Men who think in terms of people are more instinctive and honest. You're afraid of him because he isn't stodgy."

Barbara frowned her disapproval of the suggestion. "If I were afraid of him, it would be because he introduced a complete stranger to a client as his wife."

Carol went on as though she hadn't spoken. "Because inside you is this free spirit who comes up with brilliant, hooky ideas that are wild and wonderful. But you're afraid to indulge yourself completely, afraid of what might happen, afraid you'll turn out to be like your father. So you choose a stodgy man you don't love but who you think centers you and provides you with balance."

Barbara put a hand over her eyes. "I'm not paying seventy-five dollars an hour for this, am I?"

Carol ignored her. "I think you should just let loose. Stop holding back. Do this! Get a dose of John Cheney and give him a dose of you before you tie yourself forever to Trevor Wentworth."

"Trevor," she said loyally, "is a won—"

"I know. And duller than ditch water. And he gave you an IRA for your birthday. Think about it." Carol stood and turned to leave, then stopped in the doorway and turned to whisper, "Imagine what it would be like to make love for the rest of your life with a man who keeps a portable umbrella in his briefcase."

"In today's world," Barbara said pontifically, "there is nothing wrong with stability."

Carol expelled a little sound of impatience. "Don't you read the headlines? In today's world, there *is* no stability. Preparing for it isn't a virtue, it's an error. But it's your life. Have fun tonight."

CECIL AND OLIVIA Wentworth reminded Barbara sharply of the models in a bulk fiber ad she'd seen recently in a women's magazine. The stiffly handsome white-haired man and the coolly attractive gray-haired woman had been obviously chosen to assure the consumer that even elegant suburbanites reached for their product.

Barbara smiled as Cecil talked on about his stock portfolio, but she'd tuned him out some time ago. He was a handsome, older version of Trevor. His wife and son were focused on his every word. In their obvious enjoyment of each other, they seemed to have forgotten she existed. But she was more relieved than hurt.

She found herself looking out onto the sea of small tables and wondering what everyone else was talking about. She knew this sudden irreverence was directly linked to this morning's episode and her conversation with Carol. Those few moments of drama made a detailed discussion of stock premiums seem very tedious.

As her eyes surveyed the room, they stopped at a beautiful brunette in white, who was laughing as she leaned closer to speak to the man in a tuxedo opposite her. He laughed heartily in response. It was John Cheney!

"Barb!" Trevor said sharply, righting her water glass. He handed his mother a linen napkin to catch the water that was drenching her bread plate and utensils and dripping into her lap.

"Oh, I'm sorry!" Barbara's heart thudded uncomfortably as she added her own napkin to the flow. The Wentworths weren't smiling.

"What did you say about chains?" Trevor asked with a frown as a waiter hurried over to place a napkin under the puddle and distribute fresh linens around the table.

Barbara saw Cecil and Olivia exchange a quick glance, then smile politely. They probably thought she had quirky plans for later and disapproved. They didn't like her. She'd suspected their disapproval when Olivia's frowning glance kept coming back to the blue dress. Trevor's mother wore fashionable, silk, loose-legged pants and a short jacket. Very chic, very sedate, very similar to the attire of half the women in the room.

"Chen—*ey,*" she corrected. "John Cheney. My boss." She pointed across the room, trying to appear casual about the situation. "Right over there with the woman in white."

"Ah." The woman turned in their direction. Trevor smiled and waved. "Sandra Ryder," he said. "Manager of our Yachatz branch."

The woman waved back, then Cheney, following her gaze, noticed Barbara and waved also. She returned the greeting, then quickly gave her companions her full attention.

This evening wasn't going at all the way she'd hoped. She wanted her feelings for Trevor to quiet the temptation to take part in Cheney's scheme. She wanted to feel the comfortable security Trevor always instilled in her. But he was completely absorbed in his parents.

The awards ceremony was brief. Trevor was presented and applauded, then gave a speech in which he praised his colleagues and introduced his parents. Cecil and Olivia waved as though they were royalty.

Trevor was given a brass plaque and tickets for two to the Cayman Islands. "As a bonus—" the president of the bank who made the presentation smiled at Trevor "—we're giving you the next two weeks off to get in some deep-sea fishing. Our limo will take you to the airport."

There was more applause. Then the ceremony was concluded.

"The Cayman Islands!" Cecil said with the first glimmer of enthusiasm he'd shown for anything that did not involve money.

"Cecil is an acknowledged deep-sea fishing expert," Olivia told Barbara. "He gets hundreds of dollars to go out on a charter."

Of course. Barbara suspected money had to be involved somehow.

"Tell you what, Dad," Trevor said as they inched their way through the departing crowd. "I'll take you with me. We'll take off together in the morning."

Barbara saw Cecil's eyes express the same surprise she felt, that she hadn't been asked to accompany him. She couldn't have gone, of course. She had to come up with a slogan for garbanzos. But she felt there was a revelation for her in the fact that he hadn't even considered her.

"Barb's hip deep in putting a campaign together for some little client," Trevor said. "She doesn't want to go fishing. And Mom was going to leave tomorrow to spend some time with Aunt Rose in Seattle, anyway. What do you say?"

"Well . . ." Cecil made a pretense of looking to Barbara for approval.

She smiled sweetly, resolve hardening inside her. "By all means. Have a wonderful time. Trevor's right. I have work to do."

JOHN SAW HER across the crowded lobby, standing out like a moonbeam among the tailored evening suits that seemed to be this fall's fashion code.

That glorious hair was piled on her head in a slightly more complicated do than she wore to work, but he considered it a travesty, anyway. Confining hair like that was tantamount to caging a raven. And the dress. It outlined her slender curves and dipped just low enough over her bosom to force him to control a reaction inappropriate to the time and place.

Trevor Wentworth had an arm around each of his parents while Barbara led the way through the crowd. To John, who studied every aspect of the human personality in his work, the image spoke volumes. He wondered if Barbara had any idea. Barbara didn't seem as though she'd had a pleasant evening with the Wentworths. And she didn't look like a woman thrilled at the prospect of two weeks in the Caymans.

The perverse demon in him he sometimes couldn't control—and often chose not to, anyway—turned him in their direction.

Sandy tried to hold him back. "What are you doing?" she demanded in a whisper.

He had told her all about the morning's episode over dinner. "Indulging myself. Just keep smiling."

"Johnny—"

But he'd already caught Barbara's eye, and he saw something akin to a challenge in her expression. He expected her to panic as he approached, suspecting he intended to spoil her evening. But she didn't. She even met him halfway.

"Barbara," he said as they came together in the middle of the lobby while the crowd funneled through the doors. She looked truly exquisite, and he marveled that Trevor Whoever wasn't touching her possessively to tell the world she was his. "You look illegal in that dress."

He saw that his compliment startled her. Trevor didn't react. John was disappointed. Had someone said that to his woman, he'd have decked him.

John put an arm around her shoulders and drew her with him as the crowd surged forward. "Barbara, I'd like you to meet my sister, Sandra Ryder. Sandy, this is Barbara Ryan, one of my copywriters."

Sandra reached around him to shake Barbara's hand. The crowd had now spilled onto the street, and John pulled them against the outside window of the hotel as people rushed by them. The night was chilly, and the clean smell of rain mingled with car exhaust and ladies' perfume.

Barbara looked from John's face to Sandra's and found a resemblance in the glossy dark hair and the strong bone structure. But Sandra's eyes were blue, softening to prettiness the dramatic features she shared with her brother.

"Hello," Barbara said, warming to her easy manner. Then she smiled up at her employer as Trevor and his parents caught up with her. "Mr. Cheney, I'd like you to meet my friend, Trevor Wentworth, and his parents, Cecil and Olivia Wentworth." She turned her smile on the three. "This is John Cheney."

John offered his hand to Trevor, who shook it, smiling pleasantly.

Olivia said pointedly, "I was about to look for a policeman. I thought for a minute you were kidnapping her." Trevor and his father seemed to miss the tension.

John, his arm still around Barbara, admitted frankly, "I'd like to." His glance down at her was significant. "I don't know what I'm going to do without her while you whisk her off to bask in the sun of the Cayman Islands."

"Actually..." John saw a complex collection of turbulent emotions flash in her eyes. Then she said with all evidence of amiability, "Trevor's taking his father with him. They're leaving in the morning." She looked casually up into John's surprised face. "And you wanted me to help you with that special project."

Olivia turned to Trevor with a raised eyebrow.

"The garbanzo thing," he said. "I told you about it when I picked you up at the airport."

John looked into Barbara's eyes, wondering if she meant what he thought she meant. He saw vague hurt, singular determination and a gleam of daring that beckoned to his own streak of recklessness.

"All right," he said. "We'll start on it first thing tomorrow."

"John!" a familiar booming voice called from several yards away. "Barbara!"

Everyone turned toward the sound. A man appeared out of the crowd, hands in his pockets, collar turned up against the cold wind, not quite obscuring the clerical collar.

"Hi, kids!" Daniel Burger greeted them warmly. "How's my favorite couple?"

Chapter Three

Barbara, who never went to church, prayed for divine intervention. And she didn't care what form it took. Earthquake, hurricane, anything to forestall the impending disaster.

John felt his senses sharpen and the adrenaline begin to flow. This was as close as the average businessman ever got to living life on the edge. Something primitive in him responded to the danger.

He tightened his grip on Barbara's shoulder as he reached past her to shake Daniel's hand.

"Daniel, our favorite client. What a surprise," he said with real sincerity. "What brings you to the Hyatt?"

"Nothing." Daniel pointed behind him to the Gothic church in the middle of the block across the street. "Just on my way home from work."

Barbara launched into introductions, hoping to divert him from saying anything that would suggest further that she and John were man and wife.

She introduced Trevor's parents first. When she got to Trevor, she noticed that Sandra had placed herself directly beside him so that she looked as though she accompanied him.

Barbara guessed John Cheney had confided in his sister. "Trevor Wentworth," Barbara said quickly, "who received an award tonight for Banker of the Year."

Daniel looked duly impressed, and Trevor duly modest.

"And Sandra Ryder. Well..." She tried to draw Trevor away to put an end to the conversation.

But Daniel asked hopefully, "Have you given any thought to our campaign?"

Barbara bit back a gasp, then played every word over in her mind and realized there was nothing incriminating in it.

"She has," John replied. "And she's agreed to do it."

"Wonderful!" Daniel boomed. He smiled approvingly at him. "You're a lucky man to have a woman like this." Then he smiled at the group, apparently failing to notice the collective look of confusion, then started away, turning to wave. "I'll be in touch in the morning. God bless you all."

Barbara was frozen to the spot. John gave her shoulder a final squeeze, then, directly under Trevor's and his parents' gazes, he leaned down to kiss her cheek.

Barbara's heart, just beginning to slow its panicky pace of a moment ago, began to pound anew. She felt the angular smoothness of his jaw against her cheek as he held her to him one danger-defying moment longer. Then he straightened and smiled at the Wentworths as he took Sandra's hand and pulled her toward him.

"Cheney & Roman *is* lucky to have Barbara. One day she's going to be the best copywriter in the business. Nice to meet all of you. Have a wonderful trip." He winked at Barbara. "See you in the morning."

Barbara felt the breath rush out of her like air out of a punctured inner tube. Apparently accepting John's careful twisting of Daniel's remark, and ignoring the kiss, Trevor pointed his parents to the parking garage and caught Barbara's hand to tow her after him as he followed.

"WELL, WHERE IS SHE?" John paced from the door to the window in his office as Carol walked in with a steaming paper cup.

"She'll be here, Mr. Cheney." Carol placed the cup on his desk. "I told you she said she had an appointment and would be a little late. But she knows the cooperative will be here at eleven."

"It's ten fifty-five."

"But she's dependable. You know that. Here. I took the liberty of ordering you a double cap. Have a swig."

The telephone rang, and Carol ran out to her desk to answer it. John picked up the hot cup and downed several swallows. He didn't know why he was edgy. This was just a meeting like hundreds of other meetings he'd held during the lifetime of his advertising firm. He knew how to make a confident presentation and how to convince a shaky prospective client that he and Hal would give him the best ad campaign this side of BBD&O.

He'd just never done it as a married man before, and he'd feel a hell of a lot better when his "wife" arrived.

The door connecting his office to Hal's opened, and Hal peered around. "They here yet?"

The sound of Daniel Burger's booming voice came through the open office door. John looked up to see him striding toward him with the full complement of Cooperative Churches representatives.

"Right on time," John said. "You ready with the schedule?"

Hal stepped into the office and closed the door, waving a manila folder. "Ready." Then he looked around with a frown. "Where's Ryan?"

John groaned, put his cup down, then went to the door to greet Daniel, wondering how to explain that he'd misplaced Barbara.

"Good morning," he said with smiling confidence, shaking hands as the group trooped through the door.

The last member of the party slipped a slender hand in his and stopped the greeting in his throat.

In a pine green dress that clung to her bosom and waist, then flared at her knees, Barbara looked like something just plucked from the woods behind his house. Her cheeks were pink, her eyes dark, her hair— short!

Before he could stop himself, he said accusingly, "You cut your hair!"

Her eyes widened at his remark, and he realized what he'd done. As her husband he was probably supposed to know she was having her hair cut.

To his surprise she looped her arms around his neck and stood on tiptoe to kiss him. "Good morning, darling," she said, in just the right husky tone of affection.

John forgot his displeasure as her lips closed over his warmly, but too quickly. She was soft in his embrace, and his body seemed to find her nearness and the quick touch of her mouth sufficient to warrant a reaction.

She pulled out of his arms and turned to smile at Daniel and his companions. "We argued about this last night, and I suppose he thought he'd won. I felt shoulder-length hair would be neater for the photographs. But John didn't want me to trim an inch." She looked up at him, teasing and challenging him to assume his role. "Don't you like it?"

John laughed, but one of his hands at her waist pinched her lightly. He turned to the priest. "Isn't there something scriptural about a wife obeying her husband?"

Father Mike, a head shorter than John, grinned at him. "There is, but I wouldn't try to use it in an argument. There are at least as many references that tell a man to cherish his wife and make her happy."

"With a woman," Daniel said, chuckling, "making her happy usually involves giving her what she wants."

"A woman's hair should be long," Joanna Gordon offered abruptly from her chair near the desk, her perpetual frown in place, "so she can tie it back. Or short, so it doesn't get in the way." She patted her own closely cropped blond hair, then indicated Barbara's. "That length will take time and effort."

For a moment all the men frowned at Joanna. Then Hal stepped forward, placing a folder on John's desk and opening it.

"We *have* planned a busy itinerary, but it won't be so bad that you'll have to tie your hair back for wind resistance, Barbara." He pointed to the long list with the tip of his felt pen.

"I thought we'd start things off at home after lunch, since you two are in the habit of taking Thursday afternoons off." He smiled at the group as he explained. "I'm sure being followed around will take a little adjustment, and it seemed easier to begin at home where they're most comfortable."

Everyone listened to Hal intently, except Barbara, who looked up at John in horror. *She* would not be more comfortable at John's home. She'd never been there. She'd hoped they would begin in the office where *she* felt comfortable.

Under the guise of kissing her ear, John whispered, "Steady. It'll be all right."

Barbara, rubbing cold hands together, wondered what had happened to the confidence with which she'd awakened this morning. After Trevor had driven her home the night before, never mentioning John's suggestive behavior, but talking instead about the impending fishing trip with his father, she'd decided it wouldn't be difficult to give her all to John Cheney's plan.

But now, confronted with the reality of it, she began to see all the pitfalls, to wonder if her "wild streak" was finally leading her into something fatal to her mental and emotional health.

"So you'll be photographing them yourself?" Daniel asked Hal.

Hal nodded.

"Good." He smiled, apparently pleased. "And who's writing copy?"

"Barbara and I are," John said. At her look of surprise, he shrugged. "Who knows us better than we do?"

Indeed. She half expected lightning to strike him. Apparently so did Father Mike. He suggested with a smile, "Well, we know Who does, but He's not writing advertising copy at the moment."

Daniel laughed. "Good point, Michael. The cooperative has decided to send two representatives along," he told John, Hal and Barbara. "Father Mike, because he's the most enthused about what we want to do with this campaign, and Pastor Gordon, because she has the least faith in it. We thought that would help give us the best balance."

Barbara nodded, privately thinking that no combination of two people could have made the project more difficult for her—John's new priest, who was better acquainted with him than anyone else in the group, and would naturally be a more discerning judge of *her* performance as his wife, and the only woman among them, who clearly didn't like her, didn't believe in the project and would be more difficult to deceive because of her mistrustful attitude.

She wondered if it was moral to pray for help in executing a deception.

"Then the three of us will move in with you tomorrow for the next few weeks," Hal said with a confident smile directed at Barbara, "and let the rest of the scenario develop naturally, depending on what you have planned."

"Didn't you just say we're all going to the house this afternoon?" She hoped for a reprieve.

Father Mike nodded. "But I have a late-afternoon appointment I couldn't change, and Joanna has a dinner meeting. We'll come to the office in the morning to watch you at work, then we'll move in with you tomorrow night."

"If we're going to catch your afternoon off," Hal said, "we have to get this one, because next week you'll be getting ready to go to John's parents, and the following week, we'll already be wrapping up."

She smiled her understanding while thinking privately, *Rats. No reprieve.*

There was a rap on the office door, and Carol walked in with a tray filled with orange juice.

"A toast to the project," John said as she distributed glasses.

"To love," Daniel said, raising his glass. Barbara resisted until John put his arm around her and pinched her again. She lifted her glass beside his. "In its many beautiful forms. May it take over the world."

A resounding Amen followed the toast.

Daniel placed his glass on the wet bar in the corner. "I'd like to confer with Father Mike and Mrs. Gordon before you get under way."

"Use my office," John said promptly. "Hal and Barbara and I will wait for you at the elevators."

The three left the office, closed the door behind them and found themselves confronted with employees looking up expectantly from desks, peering around cubicle walls, stopping in the process of message and mail deliveries.

John gave them a thumbs-up, then had to stop spontaneous applause with a quick, "Shh!"

"We'll fill you in," he said quietly, "at the next staff meeting. Back to work."

"*I* like your hair," Hal said to Barbara as they stood in a circle with John near the elevators.

Barbara remained close to John unconsciously, his size and solidity providing reassurance at a time when she was wondering what on earth she'd agreed to do. "Thank you," she said with a nervous smile. "I wish I'd had my head cut instead. Off."

John put an arm around her, feeling the little tremor of nerves under the chic little dress. "You're doing fine. But, in the future, don't make big decisions without consulting me."

She gave him an impatient look, but she didn't move away. "It's my hair. Having it cut was hardly a big decision."

"It was when it affected the roles we're playing," he insisted. "You surprised me, and I looked as though I didn't know what you were up to."

"Then you'll have to be on your toes, won't you?" she challenged. "I think surprise is a basic part of the husband-wife dynamic. The successful ones, anyway."

She was probably right, but he didn't appreciate being called to task on it. "We have to work together," he said, "if we're going to succeed."

"She did her part." Hal punched the Down button as the cooperative streamed across the office toward them. "Her remark about you thinking you'd won the argument saved your hide."

John turned to Hal with a critical frown for which he got only a bland stare in return. Then the members of the cooperative were upon them as two elevators arrived. John, Hal and Barbara headed for one along with Father Mike and Mrs. Gordon, while Daniel and the other members wished them luck and called their goodbyes as they took the second one.

Barbara, trying to make conversation as the doors whispered closed, asked Hal, "What precisely did you want to photograph at home?"

"I think it'll all look most natural if you just follow your usual routine," he replied.

"All right." John leaned against the elevator's oak bar and pulled Barbara into his arms. "Our usual routine in the elevator is to steal a kiss."

Surprise parted Barbara's lips and allowed him to kiss her soundly. For him it began as payback for cutting her hair, then for teasing him about almost dropping the ball in the office. But as she clutched at the back of his jacket with one hand and held his shoulder with the other, suddenly everything changed.

He experienced the same sensation he'd felt in his washroom when he'd opened the door and found her suddenly in his arms. It felt right. He heard a click as a light flashed near his face.

The elevator jolted to a halt on the bottom floor, and he pulled away, perplexed. Barbara, eyes startled, looked at him as though she, too, felt something that unsettled her. There was another click, another flash of light.

"Well," Hal said, shouldering his camera as he leaned against the doors to hold them open. When the priest and the minister had passed him, he winked at John and Barbara. "I'd say we're off to a good start."

BARBARA HALF EXPECTED to see Scarlett O'Hara flirting with the Tarleton twins on the veranda of John's Greek Revival mansion. Graced with Doric columns wrapped with mimosa, it stood in antebellum splendor in the middle of a plush green lawn.

"Geez Louise!" Barbara breathed, unable to stop herself from staring, though she knew Hal followed in his van with Father Mike and Mrs. Gordon. It wouldn't do to have the mistress of the house staring at her own home. "What is this doing in Oregon?"

John offered her a hand, then concerned by her distraction, caught her waist instead and swung her down.

"I bought it from a man who came from Louisiana. He wanted something to remind him of home. I got it for a steal because it was a little big for the average home buyer."

Barbara wandered toward the porch steps, still staring. She looked at the deep veranda with its comfortable-looking, natural wicker furniture, at the many windows flanked with simple black shutters, then inhaled the mimosa and felt its sweetness flow deep inside her.

"A *little* big?" she asked. "You and the children must get lost in it."

He shook his head. "I wanted something that would give the kids lots of room—inside and out. My parents live in a big old farmhouse on the beach where Sandy and I grew up. I remember feeling myself stretch as I grew older because there was room to run, room to get away from everyone else if I felt the need, room enough that I never felt confined.''

For the first time since John had pulled up in front of his home, Barbara was more aware of him than the house. So that was how a nimble mind developed—open space with room to grow. She remembered her struggles with the garbanzo beans account and smiled privately. She'd grown up in a low-ceilinged condo tucked in with thirty other residences, moved into a dorm room with four other young women and now lived in a small apartment in a forty-eight-unit complex.

John opened the door and ushered her inside. She had a quick impression of parquet tiles and a stairway worthy of Scarlett when John pulled her into the living room. It was done in shades of blue with white woodwork.

''You have to loosen up,'' he said quietly but urgently. ''You look at me as though you're terrified. Mrs. Gordon's going to catch that.''

She shook off the hand that held her arm. ''Of course I'm terrified. This was a ridiculous idea. I don't know why I ever thought we could make it work.'' She turned to look nervously through the lace sheers to the driveway. ''We shouldn't be talking about this, anyway. They're right behind us.''

''Hal was stopping for gas,'' John said, taking her arm again and turning her to him. ''We *can* make it work. You just have to start acting like a wife.''

''I'm trying!''

''I know. And you're fine when you initiate the action. It's when I do and you have to react that you panic.''

That was true. His touch, his eyes, reached something inside her Trevor hadn't tapped in almost a year of keeping steady company with her.

She nodded, shaking her hands as though that could magically loosen her whole body. "You'll have to forgive me," she said wryly. "I've never had a husband before."

"That shouldn't be a problem," he said, "if you just relax and let yourself be honest. You like it when I touch you. Let that show."

She opened her mouth to deny it, then changed her mind. It would be futile. That moment in the elevator had proven that. Still, there was a considerable difference between sexual attraction and husband-and-wife familiarity.

"It's hard to even imagine being your wife," she admitted with a little frown, "when I don't really know you at all. It's hard to look like the woman you love, when I don't know—" She stopped herself, feeling as though she'd stepped onto quicksand.

John saw the solution as starkly simple—and too tempting to ignore. "Kiss me," he instructed.

"Mr. Cheney, that isn't—"

"Don't call me that," he ordered softly, firming his grip on her. "It's John. Or whatever wifely endearment you'd like to create yourself. Now, kiss me. It'll tell each of us a lot about the other."

"You kiss me," she argued, her eyes looking everywhere but at his mouth. This was different from the experience in the elevator. This one was calculated. "It's your idea."

"All right, but you'll have to be quiet."

"I'm never quiet. It's a problem I've had since childhood. I chatter when I'm ner—"

He placed a hand at her back and pulled her to him. She came up against him, breast to ribs, thigh to thigh, and felt every thought in her head dissolve.

He studied her for a moment, a small pleat of concentration between his eyebrows. As he lowered his head, hers rose of its own accord.

Their lips met in what she supposed to be the spirit of exploration. It took him one second to show her that he did nothing so tentatively. He was confident, decisive and wordlessly authoritative.

He cupped her head in one hand and took her mouth with a tenderness that drew a response right from the heart of her.

John felt her lean farther into him, felt her lips part and her hands move gently up his back. The cool silk of her hair spilled over his hand.

He kissed her as a husband would, possessively and passionately, tongue dipping into her mouth, hands moving over her in ownership.

Barbara had never been touched with such competence. Even as his hands wandered boldly over her and his kiss went farther than a first kiss should have, she understood he was simply showing her how the woman he loved would feel.

She struggled to hold on to the reserve that put a cap on the famous Ryan wild streak. But her reserve was frail stuff compared to John's artful assault. She felt it strain and stretch.

John was aware the instant she put up her defenses. One moment she was pliant and mobile in his arms, and the next she was stiff and still.

He drew away slowly, pulling himself together. Deep inside he felt the stirring of something he hadn't known since the days before Gracie, when he'd believed in a good woman, children around his dinner table and love that grew with the passage of time. He stared down at Barbara in suspicious surprise.

Barbara didn't have to wonder why he was frowning. Their bodies had been entwined when she'd felt it—a small shower of sparks as though something had shorted out.

Even as she took a step back from John Cheney, she knew that demonstration kiss had fused something in them, connected them to one another in a way neither had expected. She felt as though she stood with her toes over the edge of the Grand Canyon.

Chapter Four

"Just pretend we're not here," Father Mike said with complete conviction that that could be done. He sat on a chair by the white marble fireplace.

Joanna Gordon sat in a chair on the other side, her watchful, suspicious eyes making any kind of pretense difficult.

"Just do what you do," Hal said encouragingly. He was testing the light as he moved around the sofa on which he intended to photograph John and Barbara.

His subjects studied each other warily. John tossed his jacket aside, pulled his tie and shoes off. Barbara quickly decided that if he went one step farther, she was out of there.

"Barbara and I take Thursday afternoons off," he said, "because it's the only day of the week where we can be alone together at home. The kids are at school or, in the summer, at day camp, and the housekeeper takes a few hours off." He settled into a corner of the sofa, one knee bent, his stocking foot propped on a cushion. He reached for Barbara.

Certain she would not survive this, Barbara slipped out of her shoes and curled up next to him. He put his arms around her and pulled her firmly against him until she had to rest her head on his shoulder to be comfortable.

"We talk about how the week's going...how we feel." John stroked her arm as she lay stiffly against him. He entwined his fingers with hers and rested them on his knee. "Nervous, darling?" he asked, his tone gently indulgent.

"Yes, I am." She resented his calling everyone's attention to the fact, but she knew she hadn't been hiding it from anyone. The best she could do was make her discomfort seem like camera shyness. "John's the showman in the family," she said. "I prefer to be behind the scenes. He once even modeled for a Mr. Saturday Night ad."

She blessed her own nosiness in going through old Cheney & Roman portfolios when she'd first joined the company. That was a genuine touch.

At least, she hoped it was. She seemed to be losing her grip on the situation. All she was aware of now was John Cheney's body surrounding her—arms and legs providing a strong barrier between her and the woman she'd been only this morning. That, coupled with the memory of his kiss, was serving to undermine her concentration.

John felt her stiffen further, though she seemed to be trying hard to play her part. He kissed her temple, a reward and a display of encouragement for their audience.

Hal stood at the foot of the sofa and shot repeatedly.

"Did I tell you your Kate Cunningham wardrobe arrived?" John asked her.

Barbara, afraid to believe what that remark suggested, turned to look at him. "No," she said cautiously.

"Yes." John turned to the priest and Mrs. Gordon as Hal moved around the sofa to reposition. "Kate Cunningham is an Oregon designer winning national accolades. She's also a client of ours. She called yesterday after Barbara left the office to see if she'd be willing to wear her fall collection. She wants it to be seen by other businesswomen."

Barbara's smile was wide and genuine. She lusted after the Cunningham clothes when they were brought into the office to be photographed. Hal focused and shot.

For the first time Barbara was unaware of him. "Really?" she asked.

"Really," John confirmed. Of course, *he* had called Kate, but the result was the same.

Barbara sat up and turned toward him, her knees folded under her. Hal shot again.

"The *whole* collection?" she asked, ingenuously wide-eyed.

"Down to belts and shoes."

She stared at him, then laughed softly. "Wow."

John put a hand to her hair, touched by her delight. The gesture was genuine. Hal's camera clicked.

"How are you adjusting to the children, Barbara?" Father Mike asked. "It must be different having to deal with two ten-year-olds after being single."

Barbara relied on what Carol had told her and what she'd overheard when John had spoken to his children on the phone. "They're wonderful," she said. "I have a lot to learn, but they're patient with me." At least, she hoped they would be.

"You mentioned an office in your home," Mrs. Gordon said, apparently having had enough of the cozy sofa scene. "May we see it?"

Hal took more photos of John and Barbara looking over an ad layout on his desk. It happened to be the Kate Cunningham fall catalog, and Barbara became excited and animated. Hal went into action.

Later she made a pot of coffee while Father Mike and Mrs. Gordon sat at the table, watching. Finding the countertop coffeepot was easy, and John, behaving like a helpful husband, brought her filter, coffee and cups. She gave him a grateful glance.

Hal, the priest and the minister left as Libby, John's housekeeper, arrived home.

Barbara saw her smile politely at the departing trio and hurry into the house, as though anxious to avoid contact.

When they'd waved goodbye to their guests, John and Barbara found Libby in the kitchen.

She introduced herself to Barbara, then studied both of them with a frown. "I want you to know right now that I'm really terrible at this sort of thing. I blush when I lie.

"I once tried to hide twenty dollars from my husband, rest his soul, when we were first married and scraping for every penny. There was this gray felt cloche hat and...well, I guess that isn't important. But the deceit lasted all of ten minutes before I burst into tears and confessed everything."

Barbara liked her already. She was tall and pretty and impeccably groomed. She guessed her age at early sixties. She hooked an arm in hers and tried to lead her toward the back door. "Good. Neither am I any good at deceit. Let's run away together—a sort of Thelma and Louise of the Coast Range."

"Who?"

John moved to cut them off.

"I thought women in the nineties were more adventurous and invincible than ever before," he scolded. "We can do this if the two of you would just show a little spirit."

He brought them back to the middle of the oak and white kitchen. Libby gave her employer a maternal look. "Lies are not an adventure. Lies are a trap."

John nodded. "In most cases, but I explained about this, Libby. The lie began to save Barbara's reputation, then the whole thing got beyond our control. But if we all do our share, it'll work out."

Libby studied him without response.

"The children are willing to do it," he said reasonably.

"That," Barbara said, "is because they're not old enough to see the pitfalls. They probably think it's a game."

"Actually, they're thinking of it as a stage play," Libby said. Then she added for Barbara's benefit, "They were both in *The Nutcracker* last Christmas. We talked about it over breakfast this morning." She sighed grimly. "I'm reluctant to say they think it will be fun. Well, Joe does, anyway."

Barbara nodded. "Figures. That's the little chauvinist, right?"

John closed his eyes and drew a deep breath, anxious to put an end to the women's reluctance and assure himself of their loyalty.

"What if I promise you your heart's desire if you cooperate?" he asked Libby.

She began to shake her head before he'd even finished. "No. I don't have to be bribed. I'll do it for you and the children because you're as dear to me as my own. I just think you're looking for trouble. This whole thing seems to have the potential for—"

"Your own Harley," John said baldly.

For a moment Barbara thought he'd lost his mind, trying to force cooperation from a woman in her sixties with a high-rolling motorcycle. Then she saw the look on Libby's face.

"Oh, Mr. Cheney. Certainly you don't mean—?"

"I do, Libby. All the extras. Everything you want. Yours when the Cooperative Churches signs the contract."

Fascinated, Barbara watched the flush of pleasure on Libby's face, the dreamy glow in her eyes.

John put his hands on the woman's shoulders. "So, will you put your heart into it for me? Will you make Father Mike and Mrs. Gordon believe that Barbara is my wife and that we're as in love as you and Peter were?"

Barbara saw resolve take shape in the midst of that dreamy glow. "I will," Libby said. "I'll do it."

"Good. Will you excuse us? I haven't had an opportunity to show Barbara around yet."

Barbara saw one large comfortable room after another: dining room, kitchen, library, the office in which they'd spent half an hour, spare bedrooms, the children's bedrooms. She noted absently that despite the fact that one child was a boy and the other a girl, their rooms were very much alike, decorated in clowns and primary colors. They had dozens of shelves literally packed with toys, deep, walk-in closets that held more clothes than she would ever own, artfully constructed bunk beds that also boasted storage, and windows that looked out onto the deep green woods at the back of the house. These were truly privileged children.

Something about that tugged at her.

John closed Jade's bedroom door and opened another across the wide, carpeted hall. He urged Barbara into an enormous bedroom, somewhat separated from another room about a third the size by two Corinthian columns, each spaced about five feet from the wall at each side of the room.

A king-size four-poster covered with a thick, quilted chocolate brown spread stood against one wall in the bigger room. A matching dresser occupied another wall, a chair stood near the bed, and a wide trunk rested at the foot. A window seat with brown plaid cushions stretched from the big room into the smaller one.

In it was a small sofa, a television, a wet bar and a fireplace. Barbara had never seen anything like it this side of *House Beautiful*. And it was more than size and the careful choice of furniture and appointments. The house had warmth and charm. To prevent herself from succumbing to it, and to show him that she wasn't affected by it, she turned and placed her purse on the foot of the bed. "I get the bed. You get the sofa."

He smiled, and she had a suspicion he saw through her pose. "A very unimaginative arrangement, but, sure, why not?"

She climbed onto the foot of the bed and kicked off the green flats that matched her dress. "And I want you to know that I can't be bought off with a Harley." She bounced a little on the bed—or tried to. He apparently preferred a firm mattress. He moved to the foot of the bed and leaned his shoulder against the post. She frowned up at him in genuine confusion. "How did you know Libby wanted a motorcycle—and *why* does she?"

He smiled, and this time the gesture expressed fondness. "Her husband was in the Coast Guard and owned a serious hog. Whenever they got time away from the children, they rode off on it to be alone together. She has fond memories of riding on the back of it on the open road. She still has their helmets in her rooms."

Barbara absorbed that information in wonder.

"What's yours?" he asked.

She looked up. "My what?"

"Your heart's desire."

She leaned back on an elbow, and said candidly, "Leftovers."

He sat on the trunk, braced a hand on the footboard of the bed and repeated flatly, "Leftovers."

She nodded, tracing the star-shaped quilted pattern in the spread with an index finger. "When I was a child, there were never leftovers because my mother cooked only for the two of us. I never have leftovers because I buy individual microwavable meals, or individual salads or portions of things from the deli."

She shrugged her shoulder. "I want to cook for six people and have lots left over." She sighed, then heard her own words suspended in the air and thought how silly they must have sounded. She smiled a little sheepishly and sat up. "I don't know. Leftovers seem like a friendly, family thing to me."

John was both pleased and saddened by that little glimpse of vulnerability. "Where was your father?"

She slipped off the bed and into her shoes. "He was an architect in great demand. He spent most of his time in exotic locations, and my mother finally filed for divorce when I was in high school. I think he's building apartments in Tokyo right now."

John heard loneliness and loss in the quiet tone of her voice. He wanted desperately to erase it.

"Leftovers I could provide, but technically it would be Libby doing it, and I think asking you to give this your all should cost me, personally."

"Good point." She went to the window that looked out onto the lawn, the road that wound to the highway and the purple mountains in the distance. Then she wandered toward the open bathroom door.

John stood and followed her, thinking how strange it felt to have this graceful young woman in his bedroom. He hadn't brought a woman home since the children had been old enough to ask questions.

Barbara emitted a squeal of surprise. "Whoa. Three people could bathe in that tub at once."

She walked into the beige-and-gold bathroom, with its double-size step-in tub with whirlpool jets. There was a large shower, a simple oak shelf filled with fat towels in shades of brown, and a fireplace.

"Oh," she said softly, delighted to find that among the towels were two cats, curled up side by side. One was black and white and was lying on his back, two front paws stretched over his head. The other was a fat, gray tabby wound into a tight C. Barbara laughed and reached out gently to stroke each furry body. The black one stretched then settled back into place. The striped one began to purr.

"The contortionist is Walter," John said. "The one with the eating disorder is Hillary. I know it probably isn't cool to have them sleeping in the clean linens, but they show up in the damnedest places and always together."

"They're wonderful," she said, still stroking. "I always wanted pets, but I've never lived where they allowed them. Are they related?"

"No. Jade found Hillary in the woods behind the house. Joe brought Walter home. One of his schoolmates was moving and couldn't take the cat, so Joe made a deal with him. He gave him his Nintendo, and he got Walter."

Barbara's eyes widened. "His Nintendo? I've never really seen one in action, but don't little boys revere them above all else?"

John nodded and led the way back into the bedroom. "Joe will never be a businessman. He thinks with his heart. He isn't quite the unsalvageable chauvinist you imagine him to be."

From downstairs came the slam of a door that reverberated through the house like a gunshot. Then a voice shouted, "Dad?"

"Up here!" John replied. Footsteps pounded up the stairs like Hannibal's army, then two short, dark-featured gangly children appeared in the doorway.

Barbara's first thought was that they were much too small to have made all that noise. Then she wondered which was the girl and which was the boy. They were dressed similarly in blue shorts and matching T-shirts imprinted in gold with the name of a summer day camp. Both had short dark hair, wide gold eyes, and the healthy glow of well-loved, well-cared-for children.

One walked to Barbara with an interested smile, and the other went to place arms around John and study her with open suspicion. The gesture said more clearly than words could have that Jade was placing herself between Barbara and her father.

The boy offered Barbara his hand. "Hi, Mom," he said with a cheerful grin. "I'm Joe."

Barbara laughed and shook his hand. This was no ordinary ten-year-old boy. This was the wolf cub she had imagined earlier, who'd obviously inherited his father's intelligence and ready humor. "Hello, Son," she teased. "Have you done your homework and taken out the garbage?"

"No, no," Joe said. "You're supposed to ask me if I've had a good day and offer me cocoa and cookies."

Jade leaned her head against her father's flat stomach and sighed. "He's so stupid. He thinks it's gonna be fun to make believe we have a mother."

John stroked the glossy dark head. "It will. We're going to do a lot of fun things together, and Uncle Hal will be with us a lot of the time. Then we're going to

Grandma and Grandpa's for the anniversary party and to spend a few days.''

Jade was noncommittal on the activities, but not on what she thought of Barbara. ''She doesn't even look like a mother.''

''Yes, she does,'' Joe defended quickly. ''She looks like Lane Prather's mom.''

''Lane Prather's mom is a model. But she's always gone. Who wants a mother like that?''

Barbara could only side with her on that one. ''Maybe you could tell me what you want in a mother,'' she said, ''and I'll try to behave that way for the next two weeks.''

Jade unwound her arms from her father's waist and faced Barbara. ''That's the thing about mothers. You don't have to tell them things. They know everything before you say it, like when something hurts or you need new underwear.''

Joe rolled his eyes. ''She acts like she knows what it's like to have a mother.''

''I do,'' Jade said, eyes darkening with emotion. ''Becky and Ginger Goodrich talk about their mother all the time. And when I sleep over, she kisses me good-night and checks on me during the night and fixes things I like to eat.'' Her eyes swung to Barbara. ''That's what a mother does. And a lot of other things you probably don't know.''

''Jade.'' John's voice held quiet censure and a suggestion of warning. Then he turned to Joe. ''Why don't you take Barbara down to the kitchen and see if Libby will give both of you cocoa and cookies. Then you can help her bring her things in. But leave the big bag. I'll get it.''

"Right." Joe took Barbara's hand and drew her toward the door. "Come on, Mumsy. I'll tell you all about what *I* want in a mother. You don't happen to have an ATV, do you?"

The door closed behind them, and John coaxed Jade toward the window seat. The mid-afternoon sun was warm and bright. He drew the miniblinds and sat sideways to face his daughter as she plopped down on a cushion, arms folded in disgruntled displeasure.

"I don't like her," she said, second-guessing the reason for their private conference.

"You made that plain," he said, his tone mild but scolding. "She's a guest in our home, helping me with a special project. We talked about this last night."

"I know." Jade pouted and looked out the window. "I just don't like her."

"You don't know her yet."

His daughter looked at him with an expression that startled him. His endearing tomboy had suddenly become very feminine. "She's pretty," she said, her tone suggesting condemnation.

John frowned. "Yes, she is. Is that bad?"

"It's not right for a mother. You should have picked somebody else."

"I explained to you what happened. It had to be Barbara because she was involved in the whole thing. Why isn't it right for a mother to be pretty?"

Jade turned her gaze to him. "Pretty mothers don't stay."

"What do you mean?"

She gave him a long-suffering sigh, as though wishing she didn't have to explain *everything* to him. "Pretty mothers are models and actresses and news ladies on television. They're never home. The other ones that aren't those things have affairs with other men, then they get divorced, then they end up moving away and the kids have to go, too, and only get to see their dads at Christmas.''

John saw genuine concern in her eyes and couldn't for the life of him imagine where it had come from. The night before, when he'd explained everything, both children had thought the pretense would be fun. Joe apparently still thought so, but Jade was suddenly as reluctant as the other two women involved.

He pulled her into his lap and wrapped his arms around her. "Baby, nothing like that is going to happen to you. We're just pretending all this, remember? It's make-believe. Barbara's going to be with us for two weeks, then it'll be just us again."

He felt her small body relax against him as she expelled a deep sigh. "I know. But I still don't like her. She's too pretty for a mother. Mrs. Goodrich is a little bit fat, and she wears sweatpants, and her hair's short and a little messy."

John hugged her, understanding her fascination with Elaine Goodrich. He'd been room "mother" with her the previous year. Her warmth and her kindness were unconditional, and she made the best brownies west of the Rockies. But he'd discussed their situation as a motherless family with the children several times in the past, and they'd never seemed as though they felt deprived. He wondered if it was the sensitive preadolescent stage that had brought on Jade's preoccupation with mothers, or if there was something else at work here.

"All right," he said. "You don't have to like Barbara, but you do have to be polite to her. She's doing this as a favor to me, so I want to make it as easy for her as possible. Okay?"

There was a martyred sigh, then a reluctant "Okay."

"Good. Now let's go see if we can get in on the cookies and cocoa, too."

Jade leaned into him as they headed down the hallway to the stairs. "She's not going to make me do chores and wash behind my ears and stuff like that, is she?"

"I do that all the time."

"I know. But you belong to me. Or I belong to you. Which is it?"

"We belong to each other, I think."

When they reached the stairs, Jade took his hand and they started down. "How do you suppose she gets her hair to do that?"

"Do what?"

"Curl under at the bottom just a little bit."

John heard the reluctant interest in her voice. Maybe she wasn't quite as hostile as she pretended.

"I don't know," he replied. "Why don't you ask her?" In truth, he'd wondered himself how Barbara did it. When her hair had been long, it had been stick straight. Now, it looped under just above her shoulder as though it had been carefully molded to do that—yet it moved freely and glistened in the light. Women and girls, he decided, were filled with mystery.

Chapter Five

"So, tonight, are you guys going to practice being married?" Joe asked. He stood in the middle of the master bedroom in cotton pajamas decorated with dinosaurs.

Barbara turned from hanging a yellow sundress in the closet, her mouth open in momentary dismay. John stood behind him in the doorway, a steaming mug in his hands. His grin was in appreciation of Barbara's confusion.

Barbara sent him a dismissing glance, then concentrated on the child. "Ah...well...we have a lot to learn about each other in a short time."

"He's pretty much a nice person," Joe said, "as long as you do what he tells you, don't shout at anybody and don't tell lies."

Barbara's dark eyes slid back to John's, at that, in silent accusation. *The last part of that rule doesn't apply to you?*

John walked into the room and put a hand on his son's shoulder. "Thanks, Joe. I appreciate the recommendation. Ready for bed?"

"Yeah." Joe reached up to give him a hug.

John held the boy to him and offered the mug to Barbara. "Libby thought unpacking might be thirsty work." Then he wrapped both arms around the child and held him for a long moment. "Got your paints for art class tomorrow? Fed the cats?"

"Yep. I came to see if Barbara wanted to practice tucking me in."

John looked up at her over the boy's head, gold eyes filled with challenge.

"I'd love to," she said. She put the mug on the bathroom counter, then followed Joe out the door as he called good-night to his father.

"You pull the blankets up," Joe said in knowledge-able tones. "If it's been a day when I've done some-thing you don't like, you sit on the edge of the bed and explain to me what it was. You're supposed to look...." Unable to decide on the proper word, he recreated the expression instead. He drew his eye-brows together and pursed his lips. "Then you tell me you love me, anyway. If it's just an ordinary day, you hug me, tell me you love me and remind me that to-morrow I have a dentist appointment, or you're go-ing to be late from work so we're going to McDonald's for dinner."

"And how do you know so much about mothers?"

"Justin Goodrich is *my* best friend."

Of course. The redoubtable Mrs. Goodrich. Duti-fully Barbara leaned down to hug him and was ab-surdly happy when he hugged her back. "I'll be home on time to meet you tomorrow afternoon because your father will be bringing home Father Mike, Mrs. Gor-don and your Uncle Hal."

"They're going to live with us for two weeks."

"Right."

"It's exciting, isn't it?" Joe asked. "Like a play. Only *we* know what's going to happen because we're in it. I'm going to write them when I grow up and live in New York."

"That sounds very exciting. But I don't think that's a good place to have an ATV."

He blinked. "Well, everyone who lives in New York has a summer place in Connecticut. That's where I'll ride it."

"Of course. Well. Have I taken care of everything?"

"You have to pull the blankets up one more time and turn out the light."

"Got it." Barbara did as he instructed. "Good night, Joe."

"'Night, Mom," he replied.

Barbara was both pleased and concerned by his easy performance. She found Jade's door partially open and went inside to dose herself with the child's stabilizing skepticism. A Beauty and the Beast night-light glowed near the bed, illuminating the child propped up against her pillows.

"Hi," Barbara said. "I'm on a tucking-in practice run. Can I do it for you?"

"Daddy already did it," Jade said, pulling her blankets a little higher.

Barbara considered forcing the service on her in the hope of relaxing the child and herself, then decided that could be fatal to any future cooperation between them.

"Okay," she said, turning to the door. "Good night. See you in the morning."

She was in the hallway when Jade called, "Wait!"

Barbara stepped back into the doorway. "Yes?"

There was a moment's silence, then Jade asked, "Can you close the closet door?"

Barbara performed the service, remembering that as a child she'd also been convinced that an open closet door would admit nameless monsters into the room. She closed it firmly. "Anything else? Glass of water?"

"That glass of water stuff is just something you see on television," Jade informed her, curling onto her side. "Usually mothers don't like you to drink anything after you go to bed so you won't . . . you know . . . have an accident."

"Oh. Right. Sorry." Barbara tucked in the blanket where it had pulled out at the foot of the bed. "See you in the morning. Good night, Jade."

"Yeah," she replied.

In the master bedroom, Barbara found everything she'd brought with her put away, including the suitcases, which John was placing on the top shelf of the closet. He tossed up the last bag, then closed the door.

"I put the pink silk thing on the counter in the bathroom," he said. "Your toiletries are in there, too."

"Thank you." She felt a sudden, edgy nervousness as they faced each other in the middle of the room. It was dark, lit only by a small tulip lamp near the chair, and the corners were filled with shadows.

It was night. And she was about to share a bedroom with a man with wolf eyes and a lethal smile.

As she usually did, she confronted the fear head-on. "The children are settled," she said. "And I think we should settle a few things, too."

He looked more intrigued than annoyed. "Sure," he said. "I'm listening."

"Okay." She drew a breath for steadiness. "I understand that we have to share these rooms because we don't want Father Mike and Mrs. Gordon to see us coming out of separate bedrooms. And I will trust you to stay on your own side."

"My clothes," he said, his eyes blandly—suspiciously—innocent, "are in the closet on your side."

"Then I'll trust you to be a gentleman."

Despite himself, he could not sustain the innocence. A grin broke and the wolfish eyes gleamed. "Then you'll be disappointed. I gotta be me."

"John—"

He laughed softly. "I'm sorry. You looked so pious I couldn't help myself. For a woman who broke into my office and confronted me in her underwear, I thought you'd have a better sense of humor."

She turned her back to him, patience strained. "I thought anyone developing a campaign for a group of churches would have a better sense of decorum."

"You consider sexual attraction in poor taste? We're supposed to personify a happy husband and wife. We'll do a better job if we live the part."

She shook her head at his blatant attempt to manipulate her into his trap. "Good line, Cheney, but it won't work." She walked toward the bathroom, pulling the pins from her hair. "I'd never fall in love with a man like you."

He wandered after her, stopping in the doorway to lean his shoulder against the jamb. He couldn't deny a stab of hurt feelings. "Why not?"

She pulled the rubber band off her ponytail and combed the knot of hair out with her fingers. "Because you think everything's funny. You're always working things to your advantage. And you travel."

He looked at her reflection in the mirror as she brushed her hair. "Traveling is a vice? I do it for business."

She nodded, delving in her makeup bag for cold cream. "I know. My father traveled for business. The trouble was, my mother and I were at home. Eventually we learned to live without him because he was never there for us. I want a man who stays put, who'll be there. And one who isn't in advertising."

"What do you mean? You're in advertising."

"Precisely my point. No offense, but you're an advertising genius. You dramatize and sell a product. You spotlight all its good qualities and make all the bad ones go away." She spread her hands to indicate that she'd stated her case. "Advertising makes us lose our grip on reality. How can we be trusted to know what's real and what isn't—particularly how we feel?"

He found that to be an interesting argument and liked what it suggested about her. "You mean, you're falling for me beyond the boundaries of your role as my wife?"

She glared at his reflection. "No. But I imagine it could happen to a less cautious woman."

"So you've chosen this Trevor Whoever as the kind of man you want?"

She gave his reflection a scolding look as she found a jar and turned the lid. "He doesn't travel, and he's not in advertising. And his name is Wentworth."

John came into the room and caught her right hand before she could dip her fingers into the cold cream.

"You might want to rethink that," he said.

He'd caught her other hand also, and her back was trapped against his chest. She was sharply aware of his warmth and muscle and the faint, citrusy scent of his after-shave. He seemed to be possessed of some invisible snare that stole around her and held her immobile.

"Why?" she asked, her tone quarrelsome.

"Because," he answered softly, leaning down to plant a kiss just under her ear, "Trevor is traveling. He's in the Cayman Islands—with his father."

He caught her eye again, and for an instant, his gaze held no amusement. Then he leaned down to place his cheek against hers. The suggestion of a beard chafed her soft skin. "But I'm here. And I'll be just a few steps away all night long." He kissed her temple and freed her hands. "Good night. I'll be in the office downstairs for a few hours. If you need anything, hit the intercom."

Barbara stared at herself for a moment after he was gone. Her eyes were wide and a little shaken, her lips parted in surprise. Her cheeks were flushed, the one he'd rubbed against a little brighter than the other.

John Cheney, she thought, was like a sudden shock to her system.

"Yo, Mom!" Joe greeted her as he ran past her chair on the way to catch the bus that took the children to their day camp. He kissed her cheek and gave her shoulders a squeeze. "Don't worry about tonight when the church people come. Jade and I are ready."

She hugged him, grateful for his cheerful presence. "Good. I'll follow your lead."

Joe moved to hug his father. "See ya, Dad. Tonight, can we talk ATV?"

"Sure."

"Are you gonna say no?"

"Of course."

Joe smiled winningly. "I'll feed it and take it for walks."

"Cute. Go."

Jade paused in front of Barbara's chair. Barbara waited for her to speak. When she didn't, Barbara smiled and squeezed the little girl's arm gently. "Have a good day. I appreciate your wanting to help me pretend to be your mother."

Jade was frowning now. "How do you do that?"

"Do what?" Barbara asked, sure she was being accused of some terrible misdeed.

Jade put a small, short-nailed forefinger to the wave that fell from Barbara's side part and curled under just above her shoulder in a soft curve. "That curl."

Surprised that her interest was personal and purely feminine, Barbara had to restrain herself from offering an overly enthusiastic reply.

"A curling iron."

Jade nodded, still studying the wave. "Ginger has one. I don't."

Barbara said casually, "You're welcome to borrow mine."

"Come *on!*" Joe reached out to grab his sister and pulled her along with him toward the door. On the way he rolled his eyes at his father. "Curls. Geez. Who'd want curls?"

The door slammed behind them. Libby cleared their plates from the table and poured more coffee. Barbara shifted a little nervously in her oak, ladder-back chair, wondering what had ever possessed her to agree to this scheme. It suddenly seemed impossible.

John put down the financial page and placed a hand over hers. "It's going to be fine. You will be fine. Now, eat your omelet. You're going to need your strength."

She pushed her plate away. "I never eat in the morning."

He pushed it back. "That's a bad habit. You have to set a good example for the kids."

"The kids," she said, pushing the plate away again, "are gone."

"Eat the toast," he coaxed. "Bread is the staff of life."

She sighed. "Man does not live by bread alone. Let's not start quoting Scripture to each other. That would be overdoing it. What are we doing today?"

"We're going to put together the Baker Street Bookstore's campaign. Hal thinks it would be good to see you and me at work on developing a slogan and the copy."

Barbara tried to forget that she'd been alone in her cubicle when her brain had been frozen on a campaign idea for garbanzo beans. She hated to think what having three people staring at her, waiting for her to come up with something brilliant, would do to her creative ability.

She winced. John grinned. "It'll be fine. I work well under pressure—and, come to think of it, so do you. You saved Barnett with the copy for Churchill Charters' ad."

Barbara blinked, surprised he knew about that.

"I know what's going on," he said. "I'd come in late one night to finish up a presentation to Petrie Shoes and saw you hard at it in your cubicle. I stopped in the doorway, intending to say hello, but you were so deep in concentration I didn't want to disturb you. Then I saw the copy flow right off your fingers onto the screen. You had kicked off your shoes, as I recall, and had your feet up on the desk and the keyboard in your lap."

"I don't suppose Barnett gave me credit for it."

"Never mentioned you."

She shook her head and shrugged with reluctant acceptance. "That's the lot of mid-level women in corporate America."

"Not at Cheney & Roman," John said. "Barnett's moving to production next week."

Barbara stared in surprise.

"We gave him the option of moving to production or taking a hike. He chose to stay, but I'm sure it's just until he lines up another job."

"I'm sorry."

"You shouldn't be. Come on. We have to get going. Take the toast with you."

Barbara took the triangle of wheat toast with her to make him happy—and because he'd backed her even before he'd needed her for this project. Something about that warmed her and made her want to cooperate even in this small way.

It didn't, she told herself firmly, mean anything else.

"WE COULD PLAY on the obvious Baker Street connection to Sherlock Holmes," John said from the depths of his high-backed desk chair.

"Right. That's what comes to mind first." Barbara stopped pacing across the office and stopped at the bar to pour a cup of coffee. "I was thinking of playing off *baker*. You know, cooking and heat and time running out. 'You'll find potboiler mysteries, sizzling romance, recipes for dinner and for life at Baker Street Books.' Something like that."

John raised an eyebrow and nodded. "Or we could mess with the alliteration—Baker Books believes in Brontë, Beethoven, brownies, behavior, birthday cards, bookmarks and..."

He stopped, floundering for an ending.

Barbara put the coffee cup in his hand. "Don't they have a coffee bar?"

"Yes, they do."

"Then..." She repeated part of his list. "Behavior, birthday cards, bookmarks..." Then she added triumphantly, "bagels and brews!"

Hal cheered for her, Father Mike laughed his approval, and Mrs. Gordon remained completely unmoved.

John put his cup on the desk and pulled her into his lap. She landed with a little squeal of surprise and a protest on the tip of her tongue. His eyes warned her to remember they were being watched.

She decided quickly it was in both their interests for her to play along. The sooner Hal got his pictures—and he was snapping madly now—the sooner this would be over. Besides, she wasn't entirely uncomfortable.

The shoulder of John's white shirt was soft under her hand, and its just-laundered fragrance mingled with his after-shave. His gold eyes were both amused and respectful, and his smile was warm and genuine. She found it very hard to hold out against it.

She collapsed against him with a giggle. "I know, I know. You'd like to spend hours praising me and rewarding me, but we're supposed to have this ready by Friday."

"Bagels and brews," John repeated. "That's brilliant. I completely forgot the coffee shop element in all this, and that's important. Now, what'll we do for artwork?"

Barbara smiled at Hal, pleased at being able to put him on the spot. He'd been ruthlessly photographing them all morning. "That's Hal's department, isn't it?" she asked.

"Easy," Hal said. "They have an alphabet header at the front of each aisle. We'll photograph the *B* in front of the long aisle, caption with your brilliant copy, then say something about when the reader is finished with that, there are twenty-five more letters in the alphabet."

"Then they can start over again," Barbara said, sitting up in John's lap as inspiration struck her. She placed her hands on his shoulders and added with enthusiasm, "because Baker Books believes in bringing you bestsellers and bargains before any other bookstore..." This time she floundered, then added shamelessly, "...in the bicinity."

The groan was communal and even included Joanna Gordon.

Father Mike patted the empty cushion beside him on the leather bench. "Come and sit, Barbara." He laughed. "I think after a joke like that you need a confessor."

The afternoon went on in the same spirit. John and Barbara exchanged ideas, jokes and laughter and by mid-afternoon had the outline of a solid campaign. Hal photographed the process. Father Mike observed with interest, and Joanna, with jaded suspicion.

"Where are you going?" John asked Barbara when he returned from taking a client's call. He arrived back in time to see her shoulder her purse and snatch a file off her desk. Hal had taken Father Mike and Joanna with him to the darkroom.

"The children come home at three," she reminded him, reaching into her middle drawer for a yellow pad.

"But Libby's always there."

Barbara stacked her few burdens in the crook of her arm and straightened to face John. "Every working mother in the world would like to be there when her children come home from school or, in this case, day camp. If I truly *were* your wife, I'd have that option and I'd take it. I'm sure our observers know that."

John couldn't argue with her. "Then, I get a kiss goodbye," he said.

She smiled sweetly. "No, you don't. They're in the darkroom. We aren't being watched."

"Don't look now," John said, focusing somewhere over her shoulder, "but they're at the light table with Hal, probably looking over today's shots."

Barbara groaned and grimaced.

"Now, come on," he chided gently, pulling her loosely into his arms. "It isn't that hard to kiss me, is it?"

It wasn't. And that was the problem.

Without waiting for an answer, he tipped her chin up and put his lips to hers, his touch light as down and twice as gentle. She found herself leaning into him, enjoying his tenderness but craving his possessive touch.

"You did well today," he whispered, then kissed her earlobe, causing a ripple that ran all the way to her toes. "Professionally *and* theatrically." He placed his lips to the other side of her face and nipped gently at her other lobe. "You're a quick thinker, Barbara. And a good sport."

She rubbed her cheek against his and felt the suggestion of late-afternoon beard. It was a delicious rasp against her own smoothness. She found herself wondering what it would feel like against the bare skin of her shoulder, her breast.

She pushed away from him and cleared her throat. "That ought to be convincing enough," she said and turned to leave. The first thing she noticed as she walked out of her cubicle and onto the floor was that there was no one at the light table. There had never *been* anyone at the light table. She turned to John, indignation flushing her cheeks.

He winked. "Gotcha," he said, walking away. "See you at dinner."

Barbara would have followed him and told him what she thought of his tactics, but one of the copywriters was already running toward him, waving a sheet of paper.

BARBARA SAT in the middle of the bed, looking through a box of costume jewelry she'd brought with her, hoping she hadn't forgotten the crystal star she always wore on her black dress, when Joe and Jade appeared in the doorway.

"Yo, Mom!" Joe said, putting a knee on the trunk where his father had sat the night before. "How'd it go today? Did you make everyone believe you're married to Dad?"

"I was pretty convincing," she said, pushing the box toward Jade as she noticed her interest in it. "But I think Mrs. Gordon doesn't quite believe us."

Joe nodded as though he knew all about her. "The grumpy lady."

Barbara straightened and said in mild reproof, "I don't think she's grumpy, she's just . . . I don't know. Lonely, maybe. Did your father say she was grumpy?"

"Uncle Hal did. He called Libby just now to tell her Dad said they'd be half an hour later than usual. Libby told me." He pushed to his feet and went to the door. "It's time for Combat reruns. Want to come watch?"

Barbara shook her head reluctantly. It was the first time in the last few days she'd been invited to do something rather than been coerced. "Thanks. But I have a few more things to put away."

With a blown kiss he disappeared into the hallway then thundered down the stairs like a three-hundred-pound tackle.

"A mother," Jade said judiciously, sitting on the edge of the bed and fingering the things in the box, "is supposed to meet us at the bus so we're not stolen by a crazy person."

"But your father let you go to the bus on your own this morning," Barbara said, carrying her things to the dresser. She peered into the small drawers at the top for a place to put her box. They were filled with socks, handkerchiefs and a black velvet envelope she guessed held cuff links or tie tacks.

"That's because Becky and Ginger's mom waits there with us in the morning." Jade pulled open the sock drawer, then a wider one at the bottom that held underwear and methodically dropped all the socks into the other drawer.

Barbara, realizing she was probably being too hopeful, took the small action as a gesture of friendship.

"Thank you," she said, trying not to frighten the child with effusive gratitude. "Well, as I said last night, I have no kids of my own, so I'll need a little help figuring out what to do."

"First of all," Jade said, following Barbara back to the bed, "you never call us 'kids.' You say 'my children,' like it's a holy word or something." She closed her eyes and said it reverently, enunciating and rolling the *r*. "I'm not sure why, but Mrs. Goodrich always says, 'my children,' and she's about the best mom around."

Mrs. Goodrich again. Barbara sat on the bed, and seeing Jade's eyes go to the small pile of jewelry she'd left there, she scooped it up and offered it to her. Jade cupped both hands and took it.

"What makes Ginger and Becky's mom the best?"

Jade studied the crystal star, the gold hoops with three little crystal drops, the jeweled watch Barbara never wore to work. "One day," she said absently as she studied each piece a second time, "she chased the school bus down and got out of her car at a red light with Ginger's lunch 'cause she'd forgotten it. Ginger forgets everything. Mrs. Goodrich comes to all the volleyball games, she sews their Sunday clothes, and she makes the best brownies."

Jade sighed and held up the gold hoops. "I wish I had a pair of these."

"They are pretty, aren't they?" Barbara said. "But I think they'd be a little big for you. Smaller earrings would be nice, though, if you had your ears pierced."

"Dad won't let me." Jade handed the sparkling little pile back to Barbara, then added with a reluctantly accepting smile, "He says I'm perfect just the way I am."

Barbara smiled. "Well, that's true. But I think men don't always understand that women who are already pretty like to wear things that make them feel even prettier."

Jade looked at her closely. "Yeah," she said after a moment. "Do you really think I could use it?"

Barbara was momentarily lost. "Use what?"

"Your curling iron."

"Oh. Yes, sure. It's in the drawer in the bathroom."

Jade stood and put a hand shyly to her hair. "Do you think my hair's too short to make curls?" The gesture was purely feminine and Barbara felt something connect between them.

"No. Come on." Barbara headed for the bathroom and waved for her to follow. She pulled the tool out of the drawer. "Here it is."

Jade stood beside Barbara at the counter and looked at her in the mirror, raising a finger to point at the wave that fell from her side part. "I'd like to let my hair grow until it could do that." Then she smiled as Barbara plugged in the curling iron and set the control.

Barbara felt as proud as though she'd personally brought peace to the Middle East.

Chapter Six

"Look, Mom! Dad's home." Joe made a dramatic production of his father's return. Barbara decided she would have to discuss with Joe the power of subtlety.

Mercifully, Father Mike and Joanna Gordon didn't seem to notice his center-stage behavior.

Jade, hair frothy with curls, elbowed Barbara. "You'd better kiss Daddy hello," she whispered. "And call him 'sweetheart' or something."

Reluctant but resigned, Barbara went to John while Joe playfully sparred with Hal.

"Hi, darling," she said, her eyes warning him not to take advantage of her approach. "How was your afternoon?"

He pulled her into his arms and kissed her soundly, his firm grip reminding her not to struggle. When she looked up at him with disapproval, his golden gaze flashed and he dipped her backward, kissing her again. The priest and the children laughed, Hal focused and shot, and Mrs. Gordon looked away in apparent disgust.

"Good," he said, lifting her upright. "How was yours?"

"Fine." Her eyes promised revenge even as she smiled for the observers and tucked her arm in his. She hated that he could put her in a dither so easily when she was trying so hard to lend her performance some semblance of style.

"We curled my hair," Jade said, putting her thumb and forefinger to a short ringlet. "Do you like it? Isn't it pretty?"

John looked down at his daughter and put a hand to the curly mass atop her head. "It's very pretty," he said. "But, then, you'd be very pretty without hair, never mind without curls."

Jade laughed and went to show Hal.

Barbara saw John's gaze wander after her with a mystified frown. She recognized the look as a father's first realization that his child was female, and would one day be taken from him by another male.

He looked so startled that Barbara found herself assuming her role as hostess with the gracious hospitality of the real Mrs. Cheney—had there been one.

"Welcome, Mrs. Gordon," she said, smiling determinedly into the woman's grave expression. The day before, she'd looked around the house with awe and interest but had now settled into her customary displeasure with almost everything. "Jade will show you to your room. Take as much time as you need to freshen up. We'll serve dinner when you're ready. Father Mike."

Barbara extended her hand to the priest, ignoring John's raised eyebrow at her assumption of control. "I understand you're fond of pasta, so I asked Libby to prepare chicken fettuccini for you." Actually, Libby had conceived the idea herself, but Barbara felt sure she wouldn't mind the fib in the interest of adding convincing texture to their deceit.

The priest sniffed the air and made a sound of approval. "Wonderful. I'm so looking forward to our adventure here. In fact—" he looked around, nodding "—I think I'll forget my vow of poverty and speak to the chancery about remodeling the rectory in this style."

Barbara laughed at his joke and hooked an arm in his. "Just in case that doesn't work out for you, I hope you enjoy your stay with us. Joe will show you to your room, and we'll bring your bags right up."

As the boy and the priest disappeared, Barbara turned to face a grinning Hal. "I suppose," he said, "I'm expected to find my own way up since I'm often part of the furnishings around here."

"Not until you've helped me bring the bags in," she said, smiling uncertainly. "Was I convincing?"

Hal pulled off his jacket and tossed it on a hallway bench. "I'd have sworn you've been married to John and mistress of this house for a decade, anyway."

"The story I gave Father Mike," John said, "was that we've been married just a few months. That's why the passion is so fresh."

Barbara followed as John and Hal strode out to the car. "You don't think passion lasts ten years?"

John opened the trunk. Hal pulled out the priest's single black suit bag. "He doesn't think anything lasts ten years. You'd have to have known Gracie to understand."

"Gracie?" Barbara took a tote bag John handed her.

"The children's mother," John replied, pulling out the remaining two bags and closing the trunk. "She went in more directions than the wind—and in a mere fourteen months. But enough about that. We're doing well. Just keep it up and Cheney & Roman will have a national reputation by January."

LIBBY LOOKED NERVOUS. Barbara, warming to her role, caught the cook-housekeeper's eye and gave her an encouraging smile.

The fettuccini and marinated vegetables were like ambrosia to Barbara. She had seconds and praised Libby with lavish compliments that were completely sincere—and contributed, she was sure, to their little scenario.

"Mom thinks I should have my ears pierced," Jade announced when Libby served baklava cheesecake.

John turned away from an ad layout Hal was illustrating on a napkin and focused on his daughter with a carefully noncommittal gaze. Then he transferred his attention to Barbara, a trace of censure in his expression.

"Really. Did you tell her how I feel about it?" he asked mildly.

"Yes." Jade continued to eat, as interested in her food as she was in the outcome of the discussion. "I told her you thought I was too young and that you didn't like the idea of me making a hole in my ear, anyway. She said we should talk to you about it."

Hal took a photograph.

John turned to Barbara. *This is it,* she thought. The nitty-gritty they're looking for. The family dynamic at work.

"My opinion," she said, "is that it isn't disfiguring. Earrings can be a lovely enhancement to a woman's impression. It's true that she's young, but there are very small earrings for girls her age. She can graduate to something bigger when she gets older."

"Can I, Daddy?" Jade pressed.

"Mom and I'll talk about it," John said, his eyes telling Barbara they would indeed discuss it. She refused to be concerned. This had all been his idea. She was just doing her part. She might as well take it a step further.

"I think we should redecorate her room, too," Barbara said. Jade looked up at her in pleased surprise. John's gaze swung slowly back from Hal's sketch. It told her clearly not to push. She ignored it. She found it stimulating to suddenly be the one in a position of power, such as it was.

"She's too old for clowns and primary colors. Now she needs something she can grow with. Flowers and feminine colors." She turned to smile at Joe. "And you're probably ready for revolutionary soldiers or signal flags, aren't you?"

"Yeah," Joe agreed heartily. "I'd like something with bikes and babes on it."

John put a hand to his eyes. Father Mike laughed, then quickly sobered when Joanna gave him a frown of disapproval.

"I'll bring home a wallpaper sample book," Barbara said, heroically holding back her own laughter. "There's a paint and wallpaper shop just around the corner from the office." She smiled broadly at John, who had lowered his hand to his mouth, where it rested casually, as though he were merely considering the situation. But Barbara knew he was annoyed. "What do you think?" she asked him.

"Is that important?" he asked easily, a trace of humor in his tone. To those around the table it sounded like playful banter.

Barbara was completely incapable of suppressing the little demon at work inside her. "Of course it is, darling. You know I never go ahead with anything unless I'm sure you disapprove."

As Hal choked, she laughed and punched John's upper arm. "Just kidding. Of course it's important. We'll talk about it later. Shall we clear the table and talk business, or would you like to move to the living room and watch a movie or play a board game?"

"WHAT IN THE HELL do you think you're doing?" John demanded in a loud whisper.

Barbara had put the children to bed hours earlier, and their guests had finally retired after a lively game of charades.

John confronted Barbara at the foot of the bed. "For a woman who had difficulty getting into the role of wife and mother, you've suddenly found your stage feet with a vengeance."

"It was all very harmless," she explained calmly, now feeling a little guilty about the pleasure she'd taken in rattling his hold on their shaky situation. "Jade was looking through my jewelry and saw my earrings—"

"I don't believe," he said with paternal authority, "that a ten-year-old girl needs pierced ears."

"It isn't a case of need. It's a case of exploring her femininity in a way that's virtually harmless. Women

wear adornments to give themselves and their men
pleasure—it's been the way of the world since Eve.''

"I don't want you countermanding my rules for the
children."

"I didn't—"

"You've never been a parent so you don't understand this," he said, "but parents discuss things before taking issues in dispute to the children. That way
you don't hurt and disappoint them unnecessarily."

She nodded impatiently. "I appreciate that. But
you've never been a *mother* so you don't understand
this, but mothers and daughters talk, and they share
things it's difficult for a man to understand. You have
an absolutely delightful and charming son...and a
lovely little girl that you're trying to make into another boy."

"I'm not—"

"Then why is her hair cut just like his and why does
she wear the same clothes?"

"It was not deliberate. I didn't—"

"Notice. I know. But I'm a woman, and I did notice. She's a girl, and it's important that her life contain feminine things. That was all I meant when I
suggested earrings."

John wasn't sure why he was so rattled. What she
said was perfectly reasonable. Libby had made the
same point to him not that long ago. He'd taken no
action then because he wasn't sure what to do. He
didn't intend to get married and provide the children
with a mother, and hiring a nanny wasn't a solution he
could live with.

He'd explained about their mother when they'd first
asked five years ago, making it clear that she had

thought them beautiful and lovable, but had other things to do. He, on the other hand, loved them with a fierceness that nothing else in his life could have replaced. They had accepted it with the ease of children secure in their position. Or so he'd thought.

But there had to be something behind Joe's exaggerated eagerness to play the part of Barbara's loving stepson and Jade's capitulation from suspicion to adoration.

And it had all happened in the space of a day and a half.

"Look," he said. "Don't turn my life upside down, all right? Just do your job without getting in too deep."

Needing action of some kind, Barbara took the bed covers and yanked them back. "Another thing that's escaped your notice is that wife and mother are not surface jobs. Good ones tend to get a little involved in their duties."

"Just remember that you're acting."

"So are you," she said. "Like a jerk. Now if you'll excuse me, I'd like to go to bed."

John considered retreat the better part of valor. While she was in the bathroom, he pulled out the sofa bed and made it up. Then she marched past him with an icily polite good-night, a trail of some floral fragrance in her wake wrapping around him. He noted broodingly that she'd brushed her hair and that it, too, floated out behind her.

He stood under the shower for a long time, hoping to loosen the tightening muscles in his neck and back. What was wrong with him? Things never got to him, particularly things that had a funny side like this farcical little adventure with the Cooperative Churches and a beautiful woman. No woman had gotten under his skin since Gracie.

Well, it wasn't his fault. He turned off the shower and yanked a gold towel off the rack. She was the one presuming too much. True, he'd asked her to put in a convincing performance, but he hadn't asked her to arrange his life as a real wife would. He hadn't asked her to interfere with his children.

Or to look and behave with such fascinating womanliness that he began to feel that his life lacked something important.

He stepped out of the stall, the faintly antiseptic smell of his no-nonsense soap mingling with what remained of the floral scent of hers. He toweled himself off roughly, yanked on his pajama bottoms and opened the door.

The coolness of the bedroom, also laden with her floral scent, slapped his face and naked chest. He needed a brandy, he thought, snatching his robe off the back of the bathroom door. He had a feeling Joanna Gordon, if she was still wandering around, wouldn't appreciate meeting his bare-chested body.

Barbara lay quietly on her side as he left the room.

Hal, in a brown cotton robe so new it still wore creases in a square pattern from the packaging, stood at the stove bobbing a tea bag up and down in boiling water.

"Tea?" John asked in disbelief, going to the cupboard where he kept his small store of alcohol.

Hal seemed surprised by his scornful tone. "I needed a brandy, too, but I'm trying to stay in character. You'll notice I even bought a robe."

John filled the bottom third of a balloon glass with the gold liquid, then went to the stove and topped up Hal's cup with it. "This account is important," John said, toasting him with his glass, "but it's not worth our emasculation."

Hal followed him to the table against the window and sat across from him with a cautious smile.

"Emasculation? That's an interesting word for you to use—I mean, with your new marital status and all."

John swallowed half the contents of the glass and waited while it burned a trail down his throat to his stomach and settled there like a friendly little fire.

"She's messing with things that aren't her business," he said, his voice faintly scorched.

"She's only doing what you asked her—what you practically coerced her into doing. And she's doing a damned good job if you ask me."

"I didn't."

"Well, I'm telling you, anyway. Jade's hair looked great, and I hadn't really thought about it, but maybe it is time you redid her room. She and Joe weren't even here yet when we put up the clown wallpaper, remember?"

John turned to him with a pointed look. "Of course I remember. She's *my* daughter."

"It doesn't diminish your performance as a father because Barb saw something in Jade that you missed."

John further sharpened the pointed look. "Jade's hair and Jade's room are none of her business."

Hal shrugged a shoulder. "I suppose. But didn't you see Jade glowing at the dinner table? She's a great kid, always has been, but tonight she felt...pretty. You could see it in her."

"She's beautiful," John said, downing the rest of the glass. "And not because Barbara curled her hair."

There was a moment's heavy silence, then Hal said slowly, carefully, "You know, you can let her be a girl, and she won't turn into Gracie on you."

Hal's incisive, insightful observations were what made him a brilliant photographer. And that same quality made him tough to take as a friend because he had no qualms about telling someone precisely what he saw. The desire to punch his lights out was almost overwhelming to John.

"You're a pain in the butt, Roman," John said candidly.

Hal grinned. "I strive to perfect all my abilities. So, what are we doing tomorrow?"

John sighed, wishing he were going to a ball game, or on an all-male camping trip. He felt a desperate need suddenly to get down and dirty in a strictly-male environment. Instead, he faced many hours with Barbara and the children. "We're taking the kids to the zoo."

Hal nodded approval. "It's hard to get a bad shot with kids and animals. In fact, I think I'd be hard put to get a bad shot of Barbara anywhere, doing anything."

John slapped his glass on the table and stood. "Well, don't sit drinking juiced-up chamomile all night. The kids'll be up early. Good night."

John pushed through the swinging door into the darkened living room, missing Hal's grin.

THE BEDROOM WAS DARK and smelled of roses when John walked silently toward the sofa he'd made up.

"John?" Barbara's voice called quietly.

He turned toward her, wondering if the subdued tone meant something was wrong. "Yes?" He stopped at the foot of the bed.

She sat up in the shadows, her fragrance moving with her. It wound around him and seemed to tighten his chest.

"I'm sorry I overstepped," she said. "I was a little giddy with success and got carried away. I'll be careful in the future."

John felt his chest tighten further. Other parts of him also felt constricted. He moved until he could reach the tops of her covers.

"No need to apologize," he said, noting that his voice, too, sounded choked. "I'm not used to sharing my children and I was too touchy. Don't worry about it. Go to sleep."

Barbara leaned back against the pillows and enjoyed the sensation of being tucked in by strong, sure hands. No wonder Joe and Jade knew all there was to know about it.

Then John placed a hand on her pillow on either side of her, and breath and thought whooshed away. He leaned down and kissed her gently.

"Good night," he said, his voice like velvet in the dark.

Certain a pounding heart would not be conducive to sleep, she curled onto her side and bade him goodnight as he went toward the sofa.

CHILDREN RAN on batteries, Barbara decided. No, that was wrong. They were plugged into some permanent source, and even in the event of a power failure, they had some kind of backup system. She'd never seen such physical or vocal energy in her life.

In the back seat of Hal's station wagon, between John and Father Mike, Barbara struggled to appear coherent, but she hadn't slept well, and she'd been jostled awake at 5:00 a.m. by the twins bearing a glass of orange juice and an itinerary that could not be filled in a week, much less a day.

Though belted into the wagon's middle seat, Jade and Joe talked incessantly, turned toward her as much as their confinement would allow. Joanna, in the front with Hal, had turned the radio up but it hadn't discouraged them.

John, used to dealing with their energy, and looking relaxed in loose, stone-colored slacks and a matching cotton-knit sweater, smiled at her. Last night's argument, then the gentle kiss that ended it, had changed something between them. She couldn't analyze it precisely, except to know that their relationship had taken another step—and that it was somewhere beyond pretense.

As Hal and Joe exchanged little-known facts on elephants, Barbara laughed softly. "I'll wake up any moment now, I promise. I've always thought myself extremely virtuous to bounce out of bed at seven when I'd really love to sleep until ten. Five o'clock is a lot to ask of a died-in-the-wool sack rat."

John put an arm around her and pulled her closer to him. "Close your eyes. You can doze for about fifteen minutes."

She tried to protest, but he pulled her back. "Take advantage of the opportunity. It won't come again until after dinner."

With a grateful little sigh, she pressed her cheek into the cozy hollow of his chest and shoulder and closed her eyes. The way she felt now, she wouldn't last until lunch.

As John and Father Mike talked quietly over her head, the children still chatting with Hal, Barbara absorbed the physical impressions of her position as sleep crowded in. But she had only a moment to feel the warmth and solidity and the firm protectiveness of John's arm around her before her eyes fell closed.

She awoke with a start and sat up. The station wagon was still and empty. She leaned down to peer out the window and saw that they were in a parking lot, surrounded by hundreds of other cars. Just ahead was a line of ticket booths and turnstiles. Barbara turned slowly, knowing she hadn't been left alone.

John sat beside her, or almost under her, in the corner of the back seat. His gold eyes were calm but a little less amused than usual. He put a hand to her back and rubbed gently. "Awake, now?" he asked.

His touch, though tender, created a sensation of heat.

"Yes," Barbara answered breathlessly, aware of the sudden electricity in the enclosed space, the sudden rise in temperature, the sudden shortage of air. "Where is everyone?"

"I sent them on ahead. I wanted to give you a few extra minutes." Then he pulled her slowly back to him, turned her so that he could cradle her in his arms and look down at her. Barbara saw a vee of concentration between his eyebrows, as though he were about to do something that required consideration. "And I needed a few extra minutes myself."

"Why?" she whispered, not because she didn't know the answer, but because she wanted to hear it—or, in this case, taste it.

He couldn't wait another moment. He'd endured a long night of knowing she was just across the room, then sat quietly in this seat while she slept against him, trustingly secure, unaware of the hormonal riot taking place within him, demanding some satisfaction.

But as her limpid brown eyes looked up into his, as they roved his face, every bit as eager for what was about to take place as he, it was no longer satisfaction he wanted but a sincere communication, an exchange of thought and emotion that would tell her all the things he couldn't say.

Her lips were soft and warm, faintly minty, and the scent of roses invaded his senses as she wrapped her arms around his neck and drew herself up to meet him.

He braced a foot on the floor, supporting her against his thigh as he felt the mind-bending touch of the tip of her tongue against his lips.

Barbara felt his mouth open over hers, and his tongue meet hers in a battle that began gently, then seemed to escalate to a life-or-death struggle. He took everything she offered, then encouraged her to offer more.

His hands moved over her with such strength and confidence, it didn't occur to her to resist. And he seemed to be leading in a direction she wanted very much to explore.

John felt her small breasts through the light knit of his sweater, beaded tips letting him know he was not alone in the sudden conflagration taking place inside him.

The high-pitched laughter of children passing by on their way to the ticket booths finally drew them apart. Barbara pushed against John's shoulders, trying to force herself back to the here and now and the task at hand—putting in a convincing performance as husband and wife. She smiled wryly at the realization that they'd done just that, but without their audience.

John, his hands still bracketing her waist, felt weak with the struggle to bank desire, to remember that the present circumstances were too complicated for him to make love to Barbara in the back seat of Hal's station wagon.

He tucked Barbara's errant wave behind her ear and raised an eyebrow at her smile. "You're thinking that was wasted with no one to see it."

The wolf eyes saw everything, she thought, but they sometimes interpreted what they saw incorrectly. It gave her a very small boost of confidence.

She braced a foot on the floor and swung off his lap and onto the seat beside him. She took her purse from the opposite corner and reached in for her hairbrush.

"I did think it ironic that we did our best work without an audience." She put the purse aside and gave him a knowing glance as she drew the brush through her hair. "But I never once considered it a waste." She dropped the brush in her purse and smiled brightly. "Ready?"

"No," he said, reaching for her as she opened the door and leapt out. He wanted to know precisely what she meant. But she was halfway to the ticket booth before he managed to lock the car and set the alarm.

He found her standing sheepishly aside as the growing line of visitors purchased their tickets.

"No cash," she said, hooking her arm in his.

"Hmm." They took their place in line and inched forward. "You run away from me one moment, then expect me to cover your expenses the next."

She rolled her eyes. "It's a measly few dollars. You gave Libby a Harley."

"Libby didn't tell me she enjoyed kissing me—just before she ran away from me."

Barbara frowned at him. "I didn't tell you I enjoyed kissing you."

"Well, not in so many words. The meaning was the same."

It was futile to deny it. She wouldn't have fooled him, and she certainly wouldn't have fooled herself. She was falling for John Cheney. And he knew it.

She skirted that issue. "You'll have to stake me to a bag of peanuts, too, and fish to feed the seals."

He bought two tickets, then hooked an arm around her as they entered the zoo. Exotic sounds and pungent smells filled the air. A warm effervescence filled her being.

"I wish I'd known how demanding you are before I proposed," he teased.

She laughed up at him, finding it perfectly natural to loop an arm around his waist. "I don't think 'Do it or I'll fire you,' can be considered a proposal, even among the most tolerant of women."

The click of a camera shutter betrayed Hal, watching them from behind a directional sign.

"Good one," he said, joining them to form a threesome as they started off toward the aviary where they could see the children, Father Mike and Joanna. A breeze rippled the small pond on their right. "You guys are getting pretty good at this. I had no idea what good actors you are."

"You think we're pulling it off?" Barbara asked.

He shrugged. "Father Mike believes it. I'm not sure about the reverend Gordon, though. She keeps watching you when she thinks you're not looking. I think she's waiting for you to slip, or break into a nasty quarrel."

Hal changed lenses as he spoke, then moved ahead of them, walking backward and focusing on them as they strolled down the shady lane.

"Be careful," John warned, laughing as Hal almost collided with a stroller. Fortunately the toddler was not in it, but pushing it. He giggled as Hal struggled for balance and finally remained upright. "That'll look good on the SAIF report. 'Photographer's leg broken when he fell over a baby stroller. The loss of his ear and right arm were the result of a roll into a lagoon of crocodiles.'"

As he spoke, a croc raised its head from the peaceful stretch of water beyond the fence. Enormous jaws revealed long, lethal teeth, then snapped shut with a force that made Barbara shudder.

The children ran to meet them and they began a leisurely and systematic study of every creature housed at the zoo. The children, fascinated by everything, slowed to a studious pace. They took turns reading every sign aloud and asked a million questions, some the adults could answer, some that required a perusal of the brochure and some which John promised to look up when they got home.

At a vendor's stand they bought hats that were comprised of fabric animal fronts and backs attached to baseball caps. Father Mike, sporting the fangs and rattles of a snake, frowned when Joanna chose a simple, utilitarian sunshade.

Joe and Jade, pleading starvation, dragged John toward a food vendor. They all ordered foot-long hot dogs and curly fries, except for Joanna, who settled for a tuna salad sandwich and a cup of coffee.

They sat at a picnic table in the shade of an exotic tree and devoured their sandwiches as though they'd been starved. Father Mike told tales from his seminary days, and Hal talked about some of the more amusing clients Cheney and Roman had dealt with when they'd first opened the office.

Barbara noticed that Joanna almost smiled once, then stopped herself, glancing around quickly as though to be sure no one had seen her near lapse. When her eyes caught Barbara's, they held for one moment, dark with envy, then went back to her sandwich. Barbara found herself wondering just what the woman's childhood had been like, or what her ex-husband had done to her to create such a cautious, suspicious woman.

"You know what?" Joe asked under his breath. He stood next to his father, elbows leaning on an outer fence looking through an inner fence which surrounded a number of lions.

John's eyes were on Barbara, wandering down the lane with Father Mike and Joanna. Hal stood aside, changing lenses.

"What?" he asked absently.

"You wouldn't be able to live here," Joe said.

That brought John's attention back to him. "Really," he said. "Shortage of legs? No tail?"

Joe shook his head. "No mate. Everything here is male and female. They're all in families."

John was shaken by that observation. "Well, you know, families take all kinds of different shapes today."

"Yeah," Joe agreed readily, but he pointed to the lioness leaning languidly against her golden-maned mate. "I know. The world's different today and all that. But it seems like when nature does it, there's always a mom and a dad. Like, maybe that's the way it's really supposed to be. Unless somebody dies or something and then you can't help it. But if you get to choose the way you want it, it works better if there's a mom and a dad."

John always dealt honestly with his children and faced their problems head-on, no matter how uncomfortable it might be for him. And it certainly was this time.

"Do you feel deprived because you don't have a mother?" he asked. "Tell me the truth, now."

"Deprived," Joe repeated thoughtfully. "That means like I'm missing something?"

"Exactly."

"Well, yeah. I mean, I've always felt like that a little bit because most other kids at school have a mother, or a stepmother, sometimes both. But it was always okay because we seemed to have more fun than a lot of them. And none of them got anything from their moms that you didn't give us—except maybe brownies."

John was tempted to smile at his son's thorough exploration of the subject, but he sensed it was too important.

"And that's changed somehow?"

"Well, maybe a little." Joe spoke reluctantly, as though he were being careful of John's feelings. "Except for the brownies and some little stuff, I didn't really notice it much. Until Barbara moved in with us."

"But she's only been here two days."

"I know. But I saw it right away. Didn't you? It's like everything's a little . . . softer or something. I like it when she hugs me."

John had little difficulty relating to that.

"When you hug us, it's like having a bodyguard. You feel like if somebody that strong loves you, nothing can happen to you. But when she hugs us, it's very soft and I smell flowers. It makes me feel like the world is a very nice place."

Joe took a step closer to him and looked up at him with that killer smile that was one day going to make a young woman give up everything she had to follow him.

"The best part about it is that when you put it all together, a kid with a father *and* a mother feels like life is really neat and you'll always be safe in it."

John pulled Joe close to his side and kissed the top of his head, completely at a loss for a response. Joe had put forth the best argument he'd ever heard for the traditional family—at least, from a child's point of view. He was grateful the boy hadn't applied any pressure on him to change things.

Then Joe completely dissolved that easy thought by adding, "So, we think it'd be neat if you married her."

Chapter Seven

"Daddy! Come here!" Jade ran out of the building, took her father and her brother by an arm and pulled them back with her. "You have to see this, Joe! It's a nursery."

Joe resisted, frowning at his father as Jade dragged them. "You mean plants and stuff?"

"No, *babies!*"

Relieved to be able to avoid a discussion of why he would never marry, John smiled bracingly at his son. "Humor her. I know it isn't the snakes, but I bet you'll enjoy it."

John certainly did. The moment his eyes adjusted to the quieter lighting, his eyes fell on Barbara cuddling a fuzzy, blue-eyed tiger cub. It nestled against her shoulder, contentedly drinking milk from a bottle she held to its mouth. Hal was taking pictures as the priest looked on fondly.

Barbara turned to smile at John, apparently enjoying the experience as much as the cub seemed to. "Isn't she beautiful?" she asked. "Jade and I are plotting to kidnap her and take her home with us."

"She's only three weeks old, Daddy," Jade said, reaching up to stroke the cub. "Her mom is sick, so they have to take care of her in here." She pointed to a pen in which another cub about the same size lay fast asleep. "This is her brother." She shared a look with Barbara. "Looks like all brothers are the same. All they do is sleep and cause trouble when they're awake."

Joe, stroking the spotted back, turned to make an ugly face at her. "And all sisters do is eat. Is her mom going to get better?"

The uniformed young man standing by nodded reassurance. "She just got a little run-down and needed time without her cubs."

Joe winked at Barbara. "I'm glad that doesn't happen to you, Mom."

Barbara took the impromptu dramatics with an appropriate smile. "Thank you, darling. Here, Joanna. You haven't had a chance to hold her."

Joanna protested and took a step backward, but Barbara placed the cub in her arms. It reached greedily for the milk as Barbara passed the bottle along, also.

Joanna seemed nervous, then relaxed as the cub settled comfortably in her arms and continued to eat. She glanced at Barbara with a hesitant smile. "She likes me."

Barbara heard a wealth of revelation in those simple words. They expressed surprise, even disbelief. And she guessed that Joanna's suspicion that she wasn't liked ran to people as well as animals. The puzzle of the grim Reverend Gordon was coming together, Barbara thought.

"You're going to develop into a very social little being," John said as the cub was later passed on to him. The cub didn't seem to mind as long as the milk came along, also.

John enjoyed the weight of the small, sturdy body and the silky texture of its fur against his hand. But mostly he enjoyed the way Barbara leaned into him to stroke the cat. Its bright blue eyes watched her as it guzzled milk.

"I think she knows me," Barbara said seriously. "I think she'd like to come home with me."

"And what will we do with her in six months when she weighs several hundred pounds?"

Barbara grinned at him flirtatiously, enjoying the moment. "She could sleep at the foot of our bed."

He smiled indulgently at her. "You thrash around too much. What if you kicked her while she dreamed about chasing antelope? We'd have to call you No-Feet Francie."

She was surprised that he'd noticed her restless sleep from across the room.

John handed the cub to the attendant and thanked him. "I think I'd better get my girls out of here before the cub turns up missing."

Barbara and Jade walked out ahead of him, hand in hand. Joe followed with Father Mike, and Hal with Joanna. John trailed along behind in the nature of an observer.

His daughter had certainly done an about-face where Barbara was concerned, and his son was completely smitten.

It was obvious she had the priest convinced she was married. Joanna was the only holdout that he could see, and even she seemed to be softening just a little.

John realized with reluctant acceptance that he was Barbara's most genuine conquest. Though he'd found her beautiful and fascinating from the beginning, he'd looked on this whole thing as a lark, a way to get Cheney & Roman national advertisers. He'd thought it could be entertaining as well as profitable.

But he could feel his attitude changing, and he wasn't sure what it meant. Or why it concerned him. It wasn't that he found it comfortable to have her around. He didn't. He was sharply aware of her every moment, and she made him think about things he thought he'd long ago decided upon. Like the fact that he had never let a woman as deeply into his life as he'd allowed Gracie.

Yet Barbara poked and prodded at his emotions in little ways—some that touched him and some that annoyed him. Either way, they *affected* him, and he didn't know what to do about it. So he found himself kissing her when they didn't even have an audience. And he found himself admitting to her that she intrigued him. What was wrong with him? What had happened to his resolve? Emotionally what he was doing was akin to ripping off his bulletproof vest. He had to be crazy.

Then she turned, still holding Jade's hand, and let everyone else in their group go past them to the snake house. She waited until he approached, then hooked her free arm in his.

"You have to keep up, John," she teased, loud enough for Joanna to hear as the woman glanced surreptitiously over her shoulder. "We'd hate to lose you."

"I had you in my sights," he said, then leaning down and giving her a swift, hard kiss. Because Joanna was watching, because he didn't want Barbara to feel smug about teasing him—because he had to. Then he pinched Jade's chin and pulled her to his other side and led them into the building.

Joe was so fascinated by the snakes that John stayed right behind him, afraid he'd find a way to reach inside the displays for closer contact. He fielded dozens of questions, and it wasn't until they were almost finished that he realized Barbara, Jade and Hal were missing. Leaving Joe under the priest's watchful eye, John stepped outside, expecting to find them sitting on a bench. He didn't.

He looked up then down the long, narrow lane to the other exhibits, telling himself that they were safe as long as they were with Hal. But what if they weren't? What if they'd wandered off separately? What if—?

Then he caught a glimpse of them through the trees. Temper flared, then relief calmed it. And the sight he saw as he cleared the leafy barrier banished the last trace of anger.

Barbara and Jade stood atop a low stone wall surrounding a pond. Mallards paddled around in the midst of many exotic ducks, and several species of geese and swans. Hal was taking photographs.

The ducks swam to the other side of the pond and Barbara followed them along the wall, arms held out gracefully for balance. Jade came up behind her, looking more like an airplane than a bird, and, running too fast, collided with Barbara's back.

There was a little screech, and a mad flailing of arms. John headed for the pond at a run. Hal fell into step beside him as Barbara and Jade caught hands, tottered for one unsteady moment, then splashed into the water. Ducks of all kinds skimmed the surface of the pond, moving in the other direction, flapping and squawking their complaints.

Barbara and Jade surfaced together like a pair of mermaids, Barbara with a water lily on her shoulder. Seeing the water was only to Jade's waist, John slowed his steps, then planted a foot on the stone wall and looked at them with severity. For all of two seconds.

They were laughing so hysterically he had difficulty holding back his own smile. He held a hand out to Jade. "Out of there," he said. "I imagine we'll be asked to leave very soon, anyway."

John placed his dripping daughter on her feet on the outside of the wall, then reached in for Barbara. She came onto the wall like Venus rising out of the ocean, water streaming from her beautifully outlined form in wet cotton.

She laughed as she placed her hands on his shoulders for balance. "I'm sorry. There were little ducklings against the wall that we couldn't see very well without climbing onto it. I didn't think—" Her smile changed suddenly to a look of concern. "That wasn't very motherly, was it?" she whispered as he swung her to the ground. "I set a bad example. Do you think I gave myself away?"

He relented with a smile. "I don't think so," he said under his breath as the rest of their party came running. "I'm sure there are mothers who lead their children into mischief. And they know that you're new at this mothering business."

"I DIDN'T KNOW zoos had nurses," Joe said. "Do you think it's in case a lion bites your arm off or something? Or a bear reaches over the fence and grabs you?"

"I think it's more likely," Father Mike replied, "they have a nurse on hand if someone falls and skins a knee or forgets to wear a hat and feels dizzy."

"Oh." Joe seemed disappointed, then smiled at the crocodile hat he held in his hand. "How could somebody forget to buy a radical hat like this?"

As the rest of the group compared hats, Barbara sat wrapped in her blanket, afraid she'd ruined the entire scheme. Father Mike didn't seem to have noticed anything, but she'd gotten a definite look of disapproval from Joanna. Then a lingering gaze of what seemed to be confusion.

She's convinced I'm a fraud, Barbara thought. She isn't sure, but she'll find a way to *be* sure before this is over—if it isn't already.

"Warm enough?" John asked, pulling her closer with the arm he held around her. Except for that instant of censure at the wall, he'd been the consummate husband and father, indulgent yet concerned.

"I'm fine," she lied, then leaned into his shoulder and closed her eyes.

"You're a little green around the gills," Hal observed through the rearview mirror.

"People don't have gills," Joe corrected.

John laughed. "You must have missed your mother's episode in the water. Seriously, Barbara. Are you all right?"

She sighed. "My stomach's a little upset, that's all."

"She had two ice-cream sandwiches and *three* Slurpees," Jade reported, as though she considered that an impressive accomplishment.

"And she finished my popcorn," Joe added.

Father Mike shook his head pityingly. "And my curly fries. Perhaps I should administer the Last Rites as a precaution."

Barbara glared at the priest with one eye as everyone laughed.

By midnight she thought he might be right. Miserable with nausea, she climbed stealthily out of bed and stood still for a moment, listening to John's even breathing across the room. He was still asleep.

Briefly she entertained the thought of what she would do if John Cheney truly were her husband. She would climb into bed beside him in search of body warmth and comfort. She would hook an arm around his waist and press her ailing stomach to his warm back....

Deciding she must be approaching delirium, she tiptoed to the door, opened it soundlessly and stepped out into the hall. The house was dark and quiet.

She looked in on the children, found them both fast asleep, then went downstairs to the kitchen in search of a cup of tea to quiet her stomach.

She boiled water in the kettle and removed it from the burner before its whistle could disturb the household. She brewed something with wintergreen that she found in a tin and went to the table to sit.

She was half-finished and feeling only marginally better when a movement beyond the window caught her eye. Even before she could become alarmed, a masked and pointed little face peered in at her at the bottom of the French doors. A raccoon!

Barbara knew Libby saved table scraps for them. She slid the door aside and watched her visitor scamper back to his companions eating from the big bowl left near the woods.

She sat on the bench on the deck, watching the gray and black of the nocturnal raiders in the moonlight. Their long-fingered paws handled the food with almost human dexterity, turning it and washing each piece in a bowl of water Libby also left for them. Their masked faces were so beautiful and so mysterious in the balmy night, she put her mug aside and enjoyed their potluck celebration. It occurred to her how idyllic this setting was and how different from her apartment in town with its traffic fumes and noise.

"Haven't you had your fill of animals today?"

John's voice startled Barbara out of her nature study, and she sat up guiltily. "I'm sorry I woke you," she said as his tall form filled the doorway, blocking the light from the kitchen. "I just couldn't sleep."

He nodded. "Too much junk food and too much excitement. Come on. I have a cure for that."

If ever she'd heard a dangerous proposition, Barbara thought, that was it. He came to stand before her in a knee-length terry robe, his bare legs apart, his bare feet firmly planted. And he offered her his hand.

It would be reckless to take it. They were alone in the middle of the night with a force between them that sizzled with a glance, crackled with a touch. John's wolf eyes suggested all kinds of things that could be fatal to a woman searching for a steady, reliable man.

Contrary to every logical thought in her head, she placed her hand in his. She could almost hear her mother saying, "No surprise, Barb. You have your father's wild streak."

John led Barbara to the canopied lawn swing, sat in a corner and pulled her down beside him and turned her into his arms, encouraging her to stretch her legs out. The raccoons turned in unison to watch them, then, deciding they posed no threat, turned back to their banquet. The clean scent of dewy grass filled the night.

"This usually works with the kids," he said, cradling her against him and rubbing her back. "You're probably just tense from the strain of acting all day long. And on top of two ice-cream sandwiches, three Slurpees, the rest of Joe's popcorn—"

"Please," she interrupted, a hand to her stomach, "it doesn't help to catalog my sins. I can't believe how ready the kids were to rat on me."

"Lesson number one in parenting," he said, a smile in his voice. "Never trust a child to be discreet."

Barbara concentrated on the strong, soothing hand running up and down her spine and couldn't imagine why she felt safe. She was in a vulnerable position with a man with whom she'd shared eager kisses and an intimate embrace.

But she felt tenderness in his touch, concern in his demeanor. She leaned her weight against him and closed her eyes. "I'm sorry about the pond," she said softly, sleepily.

"Don't worry about it." His hand moved up to stroke her head. "Jade thought it was great. And I'm grateful you chose the duck pond rather than the croc lagoon."

She smiled against his chest as she felt all her limbs grow heavy. "I do have that much sense."

"That's a mercy."

Sleepy thoughts of the pond turned into drowsy images of the ocean. "I wonder what Trevor's doing?" she thought aloud.

"Fishing," John replied as his hand continued its gentle journey from the base of her spine to her shoulders. "With his father."

Barbara felt sleep inching up her body. "He—" she yawned " —would never feed raccoons."

"Why not?"

"Don't know. He doesn't even have a dog or a cat. And you know what?" She flung an arm around his neck and pulled herself up a little higher, searching for that comfortable hollow in his shoulder. She felt his breath against her forehead as the edges of her world began to blur.

"What?" he asked in a whisper.

"If I told him . . . my stomach was upset . . ." She yawned mightily and had to hold on to the thought as it began to slide away in the mellow darkness overtaking her. "He would have . . . given me . . . an antacid tablet."

John was beginning to think he could use one himself. Barbara fell asleep, her curled fingers against the side of his face, the silk of her hair against his chin, the scent of roses driving him wild.

Every nerve ending in his body quaked with longing. He was getting in deep—he could feel it. Like a riptide, Barbara's quick wit coupled with her sweet softness were shaking his footing, threatening to take him under.

Normally he wouldn't be concerned. He'd always been a strong swimmer. But right now he seemed to be losing the will to escape. Her slender body, molded against him in nothing but a thin cotton nightshirt, made him feel possessive and protective—and very willing to let himself be drawn into even deeper water.

BARBARA WOKE to the feel of sunlight on her body. Eyes closed, she enjoyed the warmth on her face for a moment, then turned into the pillow, unwilling to relinquish sleep for another day of pretending she didn't care for John while acting as though she did.

Then she caught the tang of citrus in the pillow and sat up abruptly. She'd fallen asleep last night against the fabric of a robe that had carried the same fragrance.

The door across the room opened and John appeared in a T-shirt and gray slacks, his hair wet and smoothed into place, his smile warm and...knowing?

"You slept with me," she accused quietly, pulling the blanket up to cover her nightshirt.

He went to the dresser in a corner of the room and pulled out a graphite-colored cotton shirt. He glanced at her as he reached into the drawer where she kept her jewelry. Then, remembering his socks had been relocated, he opened a lower drawer and pulled out a pair.

"I did. You fell asleep outdoors, if you recall." He smiled and pushed the drawer closed. "Ardor kept me warm for a while, then I was afraid we'd both catch cold so I brought you inside.''

"And took advantage of the situation."

He sat on the edge of the bed and pulled the socks on. "Actually, you're the one who took advantage. You had your arms around my neck and wouldn't let go. So I took the only gentlemanly course left me and stayed with you."

Memories came back to her of the lulling sway of the swing and his hands stroking her back. She remembered feeling comfortable and secure—and very, very sleepy. She also remembered hooking an arm around his neck and feeling his breath against her forehead. He was probably right, and she'd left him little choice in the matter.

John stood and turned to face her, pulling on the shirt as he pushed his feet into gray loafers. "Afraid Trevor Whoever won't like it?"

"Wentworth." She corrected him out of habit, then leaned back against the pillows with a frown. "No, he doesn't have anything to say about it."

John raised an eyebrow as he buttoned the shirt. "If I knew the woman I cared about and with whom I'd been intimate spent the night in another man's arms, I'd have something to say about it, no matter how innocent it was."

Barbara crossed her arms over the spread and focused on his golden eyes. "Trevor and I haven't been intimate."

His hands froze for an instant on the last button, then he buttoned it and tucked the shirttails inside his pants, laughing softly. "I knew the guy didn't have a pulse."

"He's asked," she said, before he could think otherwise. "I've just refused."

"Asked?"

She gave him an impatient look as he went to the bedside table for his keys and wallet. "Men don't just take today, or hasn't that message gotten to sophisticated bachelors?"

He dropped the keys into his side pocket, then placed the wallet in the inside pocket of a jacket flung over the chair. "I've never *taken*," he said, emphasizing her word, "even before the message circulated. But I've courted, charmed and generally seduced. It's made me crazy to stand near you. I can't imagine keeping company with you for months and not taking the relationship further."

She tried not to be pleased, but couldn't help it. "Maybe I didn't want to take it further."

He sat beside her on the edge of the bed and looked directly into her eyes. "Well, maybe you'd want to with me."

She would. She did. She returned his steady gaze with her own and admitted quietly, "Yes. I would." But she had to remember her tendency to trouble. "But I'm careful because I tend to behave on impulse. I mean, witness the fact that I am here today. Anyway, I promised myself I would take great care that I had the right man before I made love with him. Love has too many consequences."

He couldn't deny that. He was raising two such consequences right now. Still, it sounded like a cold-blooded approach to such a warmhearted emotion.

"I think if you loved Trevor," he said, "your attitude would be different. You might still want to be cautious, but you'd find a solution to the dilemma damn quick."

"Like what?"

"Like marriage."

"I thought you didn't believe in marriage."

He sighed and stood, reaching for the jacket. "So did I."

She knew she was out of line to ask, but the words formed before she could stop them. "You've finally forgotten Gracie?"

He considered her a moment, then leaned over her, gold eyes bright, and kissed her slowly. "No," he said finally. "I got acquainted with Barbara." Then he straightened and said briskly, "You'd better move it if you're coming."

She sat up, trying to behave normally while thoroughly shaken. "Where?"

"Church," he replied. "It's Sunday. I think Father Mike will expect you."

"Why didn't you tell me?" she demanded as she leapt out of bed and ran to the bathroom.

John stared after her, groaning as her rounded form in the T-shirt and her long, slender legs disappeared behind the door.

BARBARA HAD NEVER attended church regularly, but she was sure a woman wasn't supposed to think about men while listening to the homily. Several times she pulled her mind away from thoughts of John to the ceremony surrounding the ancient rite of the Mass. But several times she found herself standing when everyone else was sitting, or continuing to kneel when everyone else had stood.

Jade, who'd appointed herself in charge of Barbara's progress through the unfamiliar routine, alternately pulled and pushed her, offering cues under her breath.

Father Mike greeted them in front of the church after the service.

"I'm going to miss spending the day with you four." He pulled Jade and Joe into his embrace and winked at John and Barbara. "I have to be on the job on Sundays. But be sure to tell Libby I'll be back in time for dinner. I understand we're having cheese enchiladas. I'm delighted that you came, Barbara. I take it your mother's improved."

She nodded truthfully. "My mother's great."

"Good. Well, I'll see all of you tonight."

The children pleaded to have breakfast at a fast-food restaurant.

John winced and turned to Barbara for support.

But Joe wrapped both arms around her. "*Please,* Mom. They have these great hash browns in a little patty, and muffins and pancakes and all kinds of great stuff."

Jade worked on her father. "And we're going to be gone all afternoon. You won't have to put up with us while we're at Uncle Hal's nephew's birthday party. So you should spend some quality time with us this morning—having breakfast where *we'd* like to go."

"Or you'll feel that guilt stuff parents get," Joe warned.

John looked at Barbara, who was biting back laughter. "Did you ever hear such skillful manipulation?"

She hugged Joe and shook her head. "No. I think it should be rewarded with a fast-food breakfast."

"Then you owe me an elegant lunch," he said.

"Me? I'm not the one manipulating you."

"No, but you've obviously thrown in with them. All right. In the car."

"I hope Uncle Hal gets up in time for the party," Joe said from the back seat as John pulled away from the curb. "He was still sleeping when we left."

"Mrs. Gordon says he's a heathen," Jade announced from the other corner. "She was walking by this morning when Joe opened Uncle Hal's door. She was getting ready to go to her church. I think she likes him anyway, though."

John found his daughter's face in the rearview mirror. "Why, Jade?"

"Because she blushes when he talks to her. And she watches him."

"She watches everybody," Joe said. "She reminds me of a spy. Like she's just waiting for me to do something wrong—like call Mom Barbara instead of Mom. Then she could tell the . . . the . . ."

"Cooperative," John provided.

"The cooperative, not to give Dad and Uncle Hal the account."

"I don't think she's that bad," Barbara said. "She just had an unhappy life and it makes her kind of. . ." She thought carefully for the right word and finally used the only one that fit. "Well, maybe she is grumpy. So we should do our best to be nice to her."

The car fell quiet, then Joe's voice piped up, "I'll bet she gives grumpy sermons."

Chapter Eight

John waved Hal and the children off just after noon, then went back into the house to find Barbara coming down the stairs in jeans and a soft pink blouse that was frothy and erotic at the same time. He felt his mouth go dry.

"Ready?" he asked.

She stopped one step up, putting them eye-to-eye—except that she didn't seem able to look into his.

"I thought I'd spend the afternoon at my place... you know... catching up on laundry—"

"Libby did it yesterday. All your things are in a neat pile on the bed."

Her glance bounced off him, then wandered to the ceiling as she smiled artificially. "I have to check my answering machine—"

"You did that with your remote this morning."

"Pick up my mail—"

"Carol did that for you. I saw you put it in your briefcase at the office."

She finally met his gaze with an impatient frown. "I have things to do, John. I have a life—a *real* one."

"I think you mean," he said, placing his arms gently at her waist, putting him less than a fraction of an inch away from her, "that *this* one's getting too real for comfort."

She pushed at his shoulders, unwilling to let him close that quarter inch. "John, please don't tell me what I mean."

He held firm, neither retreating nor advancing. "Then you tell me what you mean."

"I mean . . ." she began with a great head of steam, then looked into the bright gold of his eyes and had to close hers. She finally admitted ruefully, "I mean that this one's getting too real for comfort."

He closed the small distance between them and simply held her. "You don't really want to miss our first chance to just be ourselves together," he coaxed, "without children or observers?"

She wrapped her arms around his neck and leaned her forehead against his. "I don't. But what if we like it?"

"Come on," he chided gently as he held her closer. "We already do. There's no going back." He lifted her off the step and held her against him, a strong arm cradling her bottom, the other hand tangling in her hair as he kissed her.

Barbara was robbed of her ability to reason, much less resist.

He eased her down to the carpet, letting her slide along his body, torturing both of them with the passion that flared between them. He'd told her he would never "just take," but he'd be damned if he'd let her deny what she felt for him. He was satisfied to see that her eyes denied nothing.

He combed her hair back into order with his fingers. "I thought we'd have lunch in Old Town, do a little antique shopping or jewelry shopping, or whatever kind of shopping you prefer, and maybe have dinner and go dancing."

That sounded safe enough, she told herself. Although she knew better.

"Okay," she said. "I'm ready."

OLD TOWN was a wonderful collection of Italianate buildings converted to shopping malls. Quaint specialty shops had been incorporated into the turn-of-the-century atmosphere of what had once been the center of Portland commerce.

Barbara could not believe that John was willing to wander into shop after shop while she examined the wares and dawdled over interesting displays. Trevor hated to shop.

She tried on a broad-brimmed hat decorated with beads and buttons; the brim was held back at the front with a phony pink stone set in gold filigree. It made an impression of junky elegance.

John bent his knees to smile at her reflection in the square mirror over the little vanity placed in a corner of the shop.

"Is it me?" Barbara asked, turning this way and that.

"More so than the monkey hat we bought you at the zoo yesterday. Do you like it?"

"I love it. But do I need it?"

He frowned at her. "That's the last question you should ask yourself when you really want something."

She turned to him in disapproval, her luminous complexion sparkling under the gaudy jewels on the hat.

"You've obviously never been down to your last three dollars and forced to make a decision on whether to buy lipstick or a hamburger."

"That's true. But some things feed the soul, and I firmly believe you have to nourish it as well as the body to remain healthy. Particularly when your livelihood depends on your creative spark. Let's buy the hat."

Barbara caught his wrist as he would have signaled for the clerk.

"*I* will buy the hat."

"Barbara—"

"Look," she insisted under her breath, "you can throw your weight around in front of Father Mike and Mrs. Gordon, but not when we're alone."

He leaned over her and said quietly, "But we're not alone. The clerk goes to St. Bonaventure's."

Barbara rolled her eyes at his ploy. "She does not."

"John!" A plump, white-haired woman heaved into view, stopping Barbara's words in her throat. She wore a hat similar to the one Barbara sported. "And this must be your wife. Father told me about her this morning after Mass. I'm sorry I missed you both."

"Darling," John said, placing a hand on Barbara's shoulder, sending her a laughing glance in the mirror. "I'd like you to meet Nancy Webster. Nancy, this is my wife, Barbara."

"Well, where have you been hiding, you pretty thing?" Nancy asked. "John and I worked on the roofing fund together. He never said a word about you."

"We haven't been married very long," Barbara said, her voice a little feeble as she donned her role again. "And my mother's been ill, so I've been spending most weekends with her and haven't gotten to church."

"Well, I'm delighted to see that he has you. A hunk like that shouldn't be alone, particularly with children."

Barbara avoided John's eye in the mirror and smiled. "So am I. And he was about to buy me this hat."

Nancy clapped plump hands together. "Wonderful choice. Shall I box it for you, or would you like to wear it? It's perfect with your shirt."

Reckless with relief because Nancy seemed satisfied with her paltry explanation, Barbara made a quick decision. "I'll wear it, thank you."

John and Barbara had lunch on the top floor of an old bank turned mall. Under an arched window that showed sunlight gradually being lost to cloud cover, they ate salads with cheese bread and shared a split of chardonnay.

"Gracie never wore hats," John said as he passed her the olives from his salad. "She thought they were pretentious."

Barbara looked up, surprised that he'd brought up the subject. He usually backed away from a conversation that involved Gracie. The obvious reason now was that he wanted to talk about her. She tried not to appear as though she wanted to know.

"Well, Trevor doesn't like hats on women. He says they're conspicuous." She smiled, letting him know he could continue or not, whatever he preferred. "Maybe we should introduce him to Gracie. Want my boiled eggs?"

"Sure."

The careful transference of a dozen slices of egg from her plate to his took another moment. Then John took a sip of wine and asked candidly, "Do you want to hear about her?"

"Do you want to tell me?" she asked.

"No. But I feel as though I should."

"Well, don't." She dribbled dressing over her salad with a teaspoon. "Even if we...if this..." She sighed, not quite sure how to define what they had together. "I mean, we won't, because we're not right for each other. But if we were, I wouldn't have to know your secrets. Just that that was a part of your life you'd put away."

"That's a very sane attitude," he said with an appreciative nod, "but I have the children I made with her. That keeps her a part of my life even though I haven't seen her since the morning she delivered them."

Barbara started to speak, but didn't know what to say. Such a reaction to giving birth was so alien to her that she couldn't quite absorb it.

"They look a little like her. Jade, particularly, of course, when she smiles. And they ask about her from time to time. But they've never seen her. I didn't give them a photograph, so she remains a little out of focus. I think that's better for them, at least while they're growing up. What they decide to do when they're adults is up to them."

"What made you keep them, John?" she had to ask. "I mean, you had to know it would be difficult, sometimes close to impossible to raise two babies without a mother."

"They're mine," he said simply. "They were conceived in love, at least on my part."

"I'm sorry it didn't work out."

He shrugged. "It was a hard lesson to learn, but those are the ones we remember best. She was so full of life, such a wonderful free spirit." He sighed, as though still trying to banish the ghosts of that relationship. "Trouble was, when the time came to make a few important life decisions, we couldn't agree. Despite our precautions, she became pregnant. I wanted to get married. She had plans for a career in fine art and wanted to terminate the pregnancy. So we made a deal. I paid the expenses and set her up in a studio for a year, and I got the baby." He grinned as he made the correction, "Babies. They didn't see the second one on the ultrasound until she was six months along."

"Women who don't want babies," Barbara said, "shouldn't raise them to please someone else. Everyone suffers."

"Absolutely." His answer was swift and firm. "I just couldn't love a woman who felt that way. Anyway..." He leaned back in his chair and stabbed a bite of salad. "She said she didn't want contact after they were born, and she's held to that. And that's the Gracie story."

A cloud had moved over the sun and now freed it again, pouring bright light over their table under the arched window.

"But you vowed never to marry."

He put his fork down, then leaned toward her on folded arms, his smile warm, his eyes free of any thought of Gracie.

"Then I met a woman who considers me a completely unsuitable husband, and I suddenly find myself determined to change her mind."

Happy to see him free of his troublesome thoughts, she smiled. "Do us both a favor," she said, "and don't try."

"Because I travel?"

"Partly. And because I'm looking for someone more serious."

"Serious?" he repeated disparagingly. "You mean like Trevor Whoever who *didn't* take you to the Caymans, who gave you an IRA for your birthday, who isn't in advertising, who wouldn't feed raccoons and who'd soothe your nerves by giving you an antacid? That's not serious, Barbara. That's dead."

She couldn't help the laugh that erupted. And as it did she remembered that Trevor had never made her laugh and that she hadn't thought about him, except the few times his name had come up in conversation, since she'd moved in with John and his children.

John's eyes went from the laughter in hers to the sparkling hat she wore. "I'd hate to think that you'll never get to wear that hat in the future."

"I'll wear it." She studied the bright green bib lettuce and the fat shrimp on the end of her fork. "I know Trevor isn't what I want in a man, either. I think I mistook dullness for seriousness."

That comforted him. He knew Trevor Whoever wasn't right for her the moment he saw him, but it relieved him to hear her speak the words.

In truth, John was far more serious than she gave him credit for. And he was about to turn all that seriousness toward changing her mind about him.

They walked all over Old Town, arm in arm against the cooling afternoon. They bought cappuccino and cranberry *biscotti* at a coffee bar and looked in shop windows as they drank and dunked the crisp cookie.

They bought dinosaur T-shirts for the children and one for Libby that said Motorcycle Mama.

Barbara laughed as they put their purchases in the car. "When are you buying her the Harley?"

"It's on order already," he said. "Her family's having a reunion in September down the coast. They're all into bikes. She'll be able to arrive in style."

They locked the doors, then crossed the street to methodically canvas the shops on the other side.

"I was so surprised that her heart's desire was a motorcycle," Barbara said. "She looks like such a conventional, mature woman."

He hooked an arm around her shoulder, and she reached up to thread her fingers through his.

"That's because you're stuck on 'seriousness' as important in a relationship," he said. "And because you have a warped notion of what's real and what isn't. Her husband was hardworking but fun loving, and they had a great life together on his bike."

"You think she'll be able to handle one on her own?"

"She used to. When her children were home, she had her own bike, and one of the girls rode behind her, the other with her father. When the girls were both married, it was cozier for them to go to one."

Barbara tried to picture the romance of such an adventure and couldn't. She sighed. "I'm glad Libby was so happy. But my idea of a vacation would be in the passenger seat of a Cadillac or, at worst, a comfortable Jeep."

"I'll remember that," he said. "And where do you envision yourself on a honeymoon?"

"Not the Caymans."

"No."

She played the game. "Maybe...Canada. Lake Louise, that area. It's supposed to be so beautiful."

"Good choice. I've been there."

"Of course." She gave him a teasingly superior glance. "You're a man who travels."

He pulled her to him and squeezed until laughter bubbled out of her.

"THE DIAMOND HORSE CAFE?" Barbara stared out the car window at the blue-and-white neon sign. She heard loud country-western music coming from inside when a couple opened the door and walked in. She frowned at John. "When you said dinner and dancing, I thought—"

"I know. *Serious* stuff." He followed her gaze to the groups and couples hurrying into the low structure. "But it's time you loosened up."

She turned to him with a sound of dismay. "I've never done a line dance in my life!"

He pulled the keys from the ignition. "Neither have I. But the Diamond Horse is a good client of Cheney & Roman. We should patronize them."

"We can't," she said, as though certain she had an irrefutable argument. "We don't have boots."

He shook his head in mock disappointment. "You'd let a little thing like that prevent you from having a good time?"

She gave him a fastidious look. "I prefer to be appropriately dressed for all occassions. And when I look ridiculous, I never have a good time."

"All right." He turned to her and pulled her toward him, enfolding her hands in his. "Close your eyes."

"John . . ."

He leaned over to kiss them closed. Lost in the gesture, Barbara sighed and absorbed the sweetness of it, keeping her lids lowered.

"Good," he said, giving her hands a little squeeze. "Now, imagine yourself in the middle of a dance floor with a faceted light rotating overhead and couples dancing in a circle all around you."

She sighed. "Okay. I'm in the middle of the floor."

"Imagine there's a man beside you."

She hesitated just a moment. "Okay."

"Who is it?"

She focused on the face, but she didn't really have to. She was already familiar with the feelings John's very nearness evoked in her—even in her thoughts.

"You," she replied honestly.

Then she felt his lips on hers sweetly, tenderly.

"That's for giving the right answer," he said. "Okay, now focus on us standing together. What are we doing?"

Eyes still closed, she smiled as she related what she saw. "We're laughing."

"Of course. Now focus on you. What are you feeling?"

That required a little exploration. She drew deeper into herself and was surprised to discover that under the little protective shield of caution and "seriousness," she felt eager, adventurous . . . brave.

She parted her lips to explain and couldn't quite believe it.

"What do you feel?" he prompted.

She sighed, let the shield fall away and opened her eyes to admit with a smile, "Fearlessness. And my toe was tapping to the country music."

The gold in his eyes brightened as he put a hand to her cheek. He grinned. "I'm sure you grasp the metaphor at work here."

She turned her lips into his palm and planted a kiss there.

John felt his spine turn to oatmeal.

"That standing beside you will dissolve all my inhibitions," she whispered, "and erase my fears?"

He pulled her into his arms and kissed her again, slowly this time and with tender care. "Right again," he said finally. "And it will also make you realize that you're wrong about our work warping our reality. What you feel is real, isn't it?"

She concentrated on herself and realized, heaven help her, that it was. "Yes, but—"

He placed a finger on her lips. "Don't qualify it. Let it be what it is." He kissed her again, then reached beyond her to open her door.

THE OWNER of the Diamond Horse, a tall, lanky young man in fringed white, complete with boots and rhinestones on the band of his hat, came to their table to welcome them.

In the middle of the floor, long lines of revelers danced in complicated patterns, shouting and clapping to the music. A jaunty tune spoke of love found, then lost, then found again. Overhead, the faceted light John had placed into her imagination flung diamonds across the room as it turned. Barbara felt a little as though she were afloat in the Milky Way.

She was surprised to discover that the lanky young man, Colorado, had a broad New York accent.

"Cowboy clubs aren't a matter of heritage," he said with a wide smile, "they're a matter of spirit. Even though I grew up in an apartment in Manhattan, I was alway dreaming of leading a cattle drive across the plains."

He swept a hand toward his enthusiastic clientele. "They don't do that anymore, of course, so moving a partying crowd east and west across my dance floor was as close as I could come. So, you two want to try it?"

John raised a questioning eyebrow at Barbara.

She braced herself. "That's why we're here."

Colorado gave her a hearty slap on the back as he pushed away from the table. "That's the kind of woman that won the West. Where'd you find her, John?"

"In my bathroom."

"'Scuse me?"

"It's a long story. I'll tell you about it at the wedding."

Barbara turned to John with a scolding look.

Colorado looked from one to the other. "I take it you haven't told *her* about the wedding yet."

"She's balking," John said, grinning in the face of her displeasure. "But I'm tenacious."

Colorado smacked him on the arm. "And that's the kind of *man* that won the West. Come on. I'll get a partner, and just follow us."

It seemed hopeless. Barbara no sooner got the hang of one series of steps when they launched into another in a different direction. She and John were constantly stepping on each other's feet or colliding with their neighbors, who took it all in laughing good spirits.

Colorado and his partner, a shapely, leggy blonde in a snug blue blouse, short blue skirt studded with rhinestones in the shape of a horse's head, and dyed-to-match boots, linked arms with them and led them with expert, confident movements.

Then they moved away to help another group of newcomers.

"We can do this," John said, finding a place on the end of a line and trying to fall into step. Barbara, her eyes on the lineup of boots, missed a sudden turn to the side. Her body moved in the wrong direction, stopping John's momentum. They fell to the floor in a laughing tangle.

John propped his elbow on the scuffed hardwood
floor and grinned at Barbara, who lay on her back
beside him, breath coming in giggling gasps.

"Of course, no matter how intrepid we are," he said
gravely, "there's the possibility that this simply isn't
our style."

Barbara sat up to tug her shirt down. "I hope that
isn't true," she said. "I'm really getting a hankering
for a pair of boots like Kitty's."

He sat up beside her. "A hankering?"

She nodded. "Though I grew up in a little resort
community in Washington, my heart was always
leading a cattle drive across the plains." She gave him
a dry glance, then nudged him in the ribs with her elbow. "It's just that my feet don't understand that. Do
you think we could just grab a burger somewhere and
listen to music from a jukebox?"

John could not remember a moment when he'd
been happier, when life seemed to hold more promise, when every moment seemed as satisfying as it did
now.

"We can do anything you want," he said with a seriousness so sudden and intense that it communicated
itself to her and made her realize that she'd been
looking in all the wrong places for the stalwart, steady
man of her dreams.

She got to her feet and reached down for him.
"Then let's go. I also have a hankering for onion rings
and a caramel-dipped ice-cream cone."

"You have to promise me you won't say *hankering*
anymore," he said, using her hand only for balance,
but appreciating the way she took a firm stance and

put muscle behind the yank that brought him to his feet.

"I have a powerful hankering," she said deliberately, her grin a challenge, "to burst through saloon doors and cast a steely sweep of my eyes along the bar. I'd like to swagger across the floor in my lavender boots and—" She punctuated whatever was coming next with a stab of her fist in the air.

John caught her wrist and pulled her after him. "I'm getting you out of here before you try to make an arrest."

She faked a frown. "You're no fun."

He grinned wickedly as he took his jacket from the back of his chair and handed her her purse. "I can be, I assure you. All I need is the chance. Come on."

"Isn't Libby expecting us for enchiladas?" Barbara asked suddenly as John pulled into a brightly lit drive-in. "Remember? Father Mike said..."

John shook his head as he pulled into a spot. "I told her not to expect us. Hal will be there with the kids, so we're not really needed."

He placed their order with a girl in a cheerleader outfit and rollerskates, while the sound system played music from the sixties.

Barbara unbuckled her seat belt, slid down in her seat and closed her eyes with a contented sigh. "I know it's only been a few days, but I feel as though Wednesday was a year ago."

"Time accelerates when we're together," he said, turning to lean against the window. "A lot of things accelerate. My heartbeat, my pulse..."

She heaved a gusty sigh and stretched languidly. "I know. I'm such a sex goddess."

"How does a sex goddess get away with eating onion rings?"

"We don't kiss anyone."

"Ever?"

"Not after onion rings."

"I see."

She sat up, opening her eyes. "I still don't know what to do about the garbanzos."

"No problem," John replied. "I didn't order any."

"Very funny. I'm talking about the account."

"I know. But that's a forbidden subject on a Sunday evening. Do you think Mrs. Gordon is sweet on Hal?"

Barbara turned in her seat and tucked her feet up under her. "I haven't noticed, but then I've been so concerned about my own performance, I haven't paid much attention to anyone else's. But I don't think she's quite the hard case she'd have us believe she is. I think she's been hurt."

John nodded, remembering his own pain with a wry smile. "That can make you cranky."

"Has Hal . . . noticed her?"

He shrugged. "He's usually very private about the women in his life, but he told me that he deliberately tried to distract her on the way home from the zoo after your spill into the pond."

"Because he's your partner. He has as much at stake if you lose the account as you do."

"Maybe I'm crazy, but I thought it was more than that. I can tell when he . . . connects with something, when he sees beyond what's apparent. He sometimes does that with a product when we're developing ideas. He spaces out, then he comes back with this resolution in his eyes. He did that while we were talking about Joanna."

Barbara smiled, the subject of Joanna just too complicated for consideration when she was in such a mellow mood. "The children certainly love him."

"No surprise. He's been there for them almost as much as I have. He's painted nurseries with me, walked floors with them when the kids were colicky or teething, he's bandaged them up, consoled them, played with them, scolded them. He couldn't mean more to us if he truly were my brother."

There was a sudden grating sound as the skating carhop arrived. She placed the tray on the lowered window, took John's money and made change, then skated away with all the grace and style of an Olympic contender.

John passed Barbara a hamburger and a lidded paper cup.

She took a big bite of the sinfully, deliciously fatty concoction, then moaned in approval as she ate.

"This whole teen experience," she said after swallowing, "of burgers and fries wasn't prevalent when I was in school. We were all into health and fitness, eating salads and tofu and exercising with our Jane Fonda tapes until we dropped."

John toasted her with his paper cup. "What made you come to your senses?"

"An inherent love of fat and sugar, I guess. May I have an onion ring?"

"No," he said, concentrating on his sandwich.

She expected him to admit that he was teasing and capitulate. When he didn't, she tried to reach past him for one. He caught her wrist and gently put her hand back in her lap.

"I said no." He spoke with a gravity that made her suspicious.

She tried to probe for a motive. "Do I have to wrestle you for it?"

He didn't even consider before shaking his head. "Interesting as the possibilities are, there, no."

"Ask nicely?"

"You already did, and I said no."

"You certainly don't want me to grovel?"

"Of course not."

"Then why won't you share one with me?"

He sipped from his cup and swallowed. "Because of your rule," he said.

For a moment she didn't know what he was talking about. Then she remembered her earlier joke about being a sex goddess, and her rule about not kissing after onion rings.

She wrapped up her burger and placed it carefully on the cup holder on the floor, putting the cup in the hole beside it. When she looked up at him, his eyes were alive with mischief and interest.

"I could take them from you, you know," she challenged, sitting on her knees and facing him.

He put his food aside as she had done and met her gaze evenly. "I'd like to see you try."

He'd never meant anything more sincerely in his life. He'd been reining himself in all afternoon. He couldn't wait for body contact with her.

Barbara glanced at the bag of onion rings on the tray perched on the window. The only way to reach them was to lean over him. It was time, she knew.

They'd been dancing around it all afternoon, coming in close and backing away, connecting, then pulling apart, afraid that what was already fragile might be broken by a sudden move.

But she'd been living with the need for it all day. And he'd made it obvious that he had, too.

"Maybe," she said, scooting toward him until her knees were right beside his thigh and she could place her arm around his neck, "we're ignoring another solution here."

She could see splinters of brown and green in the eyes watching her, see that confident tilt of his brow almost before it happened, feel the heat that emanated from his body, the rocklike shoulders under her arm. She had to concentrate to remember what she was doing.

"What's that?" he asked, sitting quietly docile, but dangerously alert.

"Peaceful negotiations," she said. "I give you a kiss, then you give me an onion ring."

He held her away with a hand to her shoulder when she would have leaned down to offer her part of the bargain.

"No deal," he said. "I'd get only one kiss *before* you get the onion ring, then none after."

She rolled her eyes and, using his shoulders for leverage, boosted herself into his lap. "Then what's your solution?"

"We've already discussed that," he said, determinedly stubborn. "You get no onion rings."

"Really." With a superior glance, she reached over her shoulder to the shelf, snatched the bag, and tried to escape across the front seat with it.

But he already had her in his grip, and she dropped the bag on the floor as he prevented her escape by yanking her toward him. "Really," he said. "You'll notice that you still don't have them. So I get a kiss now and the promise of more afterward at every stop light between here and home, in the driveway, on the porch, and upstairs—" His voice dropped to a whisper that suggested the meaning behind his words. "When everyone else has gone to bed."

She wanted desperately to make love with him, but she knew it would negate all the care she'd taken thus far.

"But it's . . . asking for trouble."

"I know," he whispered, kissing her earlobe. "But expecting to live your life without trouble is far less realistic than writing advertising slogans."

His kisses traced the line of her jaw. When his hand slipped under her blouse, she felt the world spin. "John," she said breathlessly.

In a matter of seconds she felt as though she'd never had a grasp of reality. His lips moved on hers, reshaping her thoughts, her plans, her fondest wishes for solidity in her life. His tongue delved deep inside her, searching for the love she wanted to hide from him. He kissed her until that love flowered between them, too bright, too alive to ignore.

And all the time his hand caressed her softness, sculpting it to his touch. She leaned into him, whispering his name again.

"Yes," he said softly. "You're mine. It doesn't matter whether you admit or deny it. You belong to me, and I belong to you."

She had no clever argument with which to fight him, no brilliant plan to disarm him. The hard truth was that he was right.

And she'd forgotten why she'd ever thought otherwise.

Chapter Nine

It began to rain. Large drops plopped onto the wind-
shield, blurring the neon lights into a bright riot of
pattern and color as John drove home.

He and Barbara leaned toward each other at every
red light, sometimes kissing, sometimes simply looking into each other's eyes and seeing things that hadn't
been there the day before, things that were the product of this day's honesty.

At home, they stood in the darkness of the garage
and held each other. John kissed her, then reached into
the car for her hat and placed it on her head.

A short, covered walk connected the garage to the
back porch, and they stopped again under the light to
drink in the glow in each other's eyes. Then John took
her hand and urged her inside.

They found Hal alone in the kitchen, reading the
Sunday paper at the table and sipping brandy. His
gaze went from John to Barbara then back to John as
though he saw something he wanted to confirm with
a second look. Then he nodded and smiled, his eyes
moving up to Barbara's hat.

She resisted an impulse to hide behind John, certain the weight she felt on her head wasn't whimsical millinery at all, but her feelings for John, gathered into a formidable little pile and tied with a bow.

"Good day?" Hal asked.

"Great," John replied. "You?"

"Nerve-racking. Remind me never to volunteer to play bouncer at a kids' birthday party again. Your children are asleep, by the way, having consumed a disgusting amount of food."

John grinned. "Thanks for taking them. Father Mike and Joanna get back okay?"

"In time for dinner. They've both retired for the night. Libby, too. The weekend answering service called. Bentley-Bowles left an urgent message about some new company they've acquired. I tried to call them back and got *their* weekend answering service. I told them we'd be in touch tomorrow morning."

John groaned. "Why do we get all the clients who love to work on Sundays?"

"Just lucky, I guess." Hal looked from one to the other again with a small smile. "Don't sleep too late. Libby promised eggs Benedict for breakfast."

Barbara said good-night politely while reading the speculation in Hal's eyes.

She and John looked in on the children together, then walked into John's dark, cool bedroom. Rain tapped lightly against the windows and the roof and made little whooshing sounds in the trees behind the house.

John reached for the light switch, but Barbara caught his hand. She didn't want to shed light on anything. She wanted to capture the dark velvet of the moment and react with the reckless impulse she was tired of denying.

She loved John Cheney. What had begun as deceit seemed to have turned into the single most important truth of her life. She didn't care that he traveled and solved everything with a grin. She wanted him more than anything.

John turned the hand she'd caught so that he could capture hers. He felt hers trembling. It started a tremor in him he tried desperately to steady.

"What is it?" he asked, using his free hand to slowly remove her hat and put it aside.

She came against him in the darkness, one hand moving inside his jacket to the back of his shirt. His body reacted as though she'd touched naked flesh.

"Love," she whispered, her eyes luminous in the darkness as she said in awe, "John, I'm in love with you."

He crushed her against him, their combined heartbeats quickening the tempo of the quiet night. "Barbara," he said softly. "I've been waiting for you for a long time."

"Oh, John." She heaved a ragged little sigh and pulled away from him.

John felt a moment's concern, certain she'd decided loving him was not a sound decision after all. Then she put her hands to the lapels of his jacket and pushed it from his shoulders. He let it fall to the floor.

She worked on the buttons of his shirt, and he tried to unfasten hers, but the buttons were too small for his large fingers. So he tugged the blouse out of her jeans and she opened the top two buttons, then raised her arms to let him lift it off.

The white of her silky bra shimmered in the darkness. He placed his hands gently over her, and she closed her eyes, leaning into him. He heard her shuddering breath.

Barbara felt the electric sensation of his touch from the tips of her breasts to the soles of her feet. He pulled her to him, caressed her bare shoulders and waist with hands that were strong and sure, then unhooked her bra and pulled her away to slip it off.

The moment she was free of it she went back into his arms, pressing her breasts against the jut of his ribs. His groan and her sigh merged in the quiet room.

He lifted her onto the bed and unbuttoned and unzipped her jeans. He slipped his fingers between the silk of her skin and her undies and pulled down. She lifted her hips to help him then sat up to reach for him as he tossed jeans, panties and shoes aside.

He went back to the mattress with her, his knees straddling her waist as her hands crept up between his undershirt and his skin. The sensation was so intense, he felt as though he could discern her very fingerprints against his body.

He yanked the shirt off and braced himself as she unbuckled his belt, unbuttoned the waistband of his slacks and lowered his zipper. His body began to riot.

In moments he'd shed his slacks and briefs, then he braced his hands on the mattress as she drew them down.

"I love you," he said urgently. "Did I tell you that?" He couldn't remember. His thoughts were spinning.

"You did," she said, putting her lips to his chest and kissing a line across his shoulders. "Right after I told you I love you."

"I don't think the word is strong enough." He enfolded her in his arms and stroked every silken curve and hollow of her back. "What I feel is like—like dynamite in a teacup." His touch became more urgent. "Impossible," he said breathlessly, "to contain."

Barbara suspected her body temperature had reached a combustible level. The movement of his hands over her, touching, shaping, teasing, was acting like a match to her own explosives. Everything inside her was racing, smoking.

He turned her onto her back and leaned over her, opening his mouth on hers as he swept his hand down her stomach and dipped gently inside her.

She moaned against his lips. Her body opened for him, strained against his touch, quaked madly with the quickening of the moment.

Barbara swept her hand down his side, over his hip, then to his manhood.

Her small, firm hand ignited the dynamite, destroying the teacup, the very world he lived in, and flinging him out into the universe. He rose over her just in time to take her with him. They clung together in an orbit around the perfect world each had wanted and never hoped to find.

Landing safely, each thought separately, was going to be the only problem.

BARBARA STEPPED out of the shower into John's waiting arms with a little shriek of surprise.

"I'm drenched," she warned, pushing halfheartedly against his naked body with one hand as she stretched her other hand just short of the towel rack.

"Doesn't matter," he said, nuzzling her neck. "I'm not dressed."

"You should be . . . getting dressed. The alarm rang fifteen . . . minutes ago. John, it's Monday."

"I heard the alarm," he said, reaching beyond her straining hand for the towel and drying her back with it as he continued to kiss and nip at her. "I don't care what day it is. Where's your sentimentality, anyway? This is all so familiar, Barbara. This is how we met."

Barbara had to work to form words as he rubbed the towel over her bottom and the backs of her thighs. "I was not naked," she denied. "I was wearing a teddy."

He made a wolfish sound of approval. "I remember. It's imprinted on my mind."

"The children will be up soon," she cautioned as he began to dab at her breasts with the towel.

John looked into her eyes and saw the same desire and awe that he'd felt last night. He hadn't imagined it. She loved him, too.

Barbara watched him toss the towel aside and pull her to him with all the fevered burning emotion that had surrounded their union the night before. She felt the heat rise in her again, bringing her back to that same burning recklessness that made her see and feel only John.

"Then we'd better hurry," he said. He swept her up in his arms and turned sideways to pass through the door into the bedroom.

Barbara was fascinated that it could all be new again this morning when they'd made love three times during the night. Though his touch had become dearly familiar, and she realized she could feel it on her even when he drew his hands away, the style with which they came together now was different.

Out of necessity he moved quickly, but remembered every little detail he'd learned about her during the long night. He brought her quickly to gasping, greedy madness, then entered her with a swift thrust that sent both of them into a little corner of heaven.

"YES," JOHN SAID into the portable phone as he tried to button his shirt with one hand. It wasn't working.

Barbara, clad in a white blouse with a ruffly jabot and a half-slip, came to brush his hands aside and help him.

"Hal told me you called," he said, running a knuckle over her cheekbone. "I read about the acquisition in the *Wall Street Journal*. Congratulations."

Finished buttoning his shirt, Barbara tried to walk away, but he caught her hand and pulled her back. She gave him a scolding smile, pinching the side of her slip between thumb and forefinger then indicating the closet to explain wordlessly that she had to finish getting dressed.

She heard indistinguishable conversation on the other end of the line as John nodded. Then he slipped his hand into the elastic waist of the slip and tugged down.

She slapped at him and he raised an arm in theatrical defense while saying in the most polished business voice, "Of course. We'll want to move on that right away."

Smiling, Barbara went to the closet and pulled on a simple, pin-striped skirt. She wondered if Bentley-Bowles's new company would mean a temporary halt to the development of the cooperative's program. When Cheney & Roman developed a new campaign, John worked tirelessly with the client, according to Carol, inspecting all their products and listening to all their ideas. This part of a project would not allow the observance of Father Mike and Pastor Gordon.

Bowles's offices, she knew, were in one of the new buildings by the river, so even if John had to be out of the office during the day, she'd still have him at night. And right now she wouldn't complain about anything that lengthened this time they had together.

"No, I don't know a lot about them," John said into the phone, wandering across the room to the window. "Rubber products, I believe the article said. Everything from bar mats to parts for the F14."

Barbara pulled her matching jacket out of the closet and looked around the room for her purse.

"I missed that part," John said. "Where is their plant?"

Barbara heard the small silence and knew instantly what it meant. She turned from her search behind the chair next to the bed, hair rumpled, and looked into John's eyes.

His gaze held hers steadily. "Rhode Island," he said. "You couldn't have acquired something in Washington or California?"

Barbara heard the laughter on the other end of the line and wanted to throttle John and the president of Bentley-Bowles.

She calmly resumed her search. So much for her cozy little scenario of John coming home to her every night. He was going to be thirty-three hundred miles away.

"Yes, I can," John was saying. "I can lay a good foundation in a few days, but I have to be home for a personal obligation at the end of the week. If necessary, I'll return later for details." He listened for a moment. Barbara felt his eyes follow her around the room as she lifted the dust ruffle and peered under the bed. "Good. I'll leave this afternoon and be there first thing in the morning."

She saw nothing, not even dust. She surfaced, her hair falling over her eyes, to find herself nose to lens with a camera. Hal, one knee braced on the foot of the bed, took the picture.

She gave him a moue of disapproval. "Is nothing sacred?"

He shook his head. "Your door was open and I saw that you were dressed, so I followed the cats in." He pointed to the tuxedo and the tabby who must have wandered in while she was distracted by the search for her purse. They were curled up together on John's pillow. "I figured you might pay me to destroy that shot. All photographers have a blackmail file for when times get lean."

She pushed him aside and went past him. "I don't think Mrs. Gordon would approve."

"I believe she considers me a lost cause, anyway."

Barbara passed John, still on the phone. He reached out to touch her cheek. Hal photographed the action.

Barbara drew away without meeting John's eyes to check the bathroom. The spark with which she'd awakened this morning was sputtering dangerously, and she wanted to keep the feeling to herself until she understood it.

She heard John terminate the call, then palm down the phone's antenna. Then he demanded of Hal, "What are you doing in our bedroom?"

"It's on our schedule of shots," Hal replied. Barbara heard the rustle of paper. "See? Right here. 'Preparation for work.' What'd Bentley say? You off to the new company?"

"Yeah. It's in Rhode Island."

Hal whistled. "You need me?"

"No. You'd better make sure everything runs smoothly here. We'll go back together after I figure out what they want. Now, will you beat it so we can finish getting ready?"

"Right."

The bedroom door closed.

Barbara was now in the closet, checking the cedar shelves, parting clothes to check the floor.

"I'll be home by Thursday," John said from right behind her. When she didn't reply, he reached in and pulled her out.

"Yes, I know," she said and moved past him to check underneath the nightstand.

"Barbara," he said, his tone exasperated. He pulled her to her feet and lifted her chin until she was forced to look at him. "Don't confuse me with your father. I'll be thinking about you all the time I'm gone."

She sighed and raised her hands to his arms. "I know. I understand that you have to go."

He sat on the edge of the bed and pulled her onto his lap. "Then, what are you upset about?"

She looped her arms around his neck and ran her thumb gently along his jawline. "Because I woke up, still glowing from making love with you—and then there was Hal with his camera, and I remembered that we're just like the actors in the coffee commercial."

"You know that isn't true," he said, squeezing her to him. "It began that way, but now it's real."

She looked into his eyes, hers wide and troubled. "Do you know what's real? How much of this is what you feel for me, and how much is just advertising entangled with your home life? Is this just my wild Ryan streak kicking in, loving the danger, wanting to stretch it to its limit?" Her voice quieted and she lowered her eyes. "Do you really love *me*, or do I just represent the rounding out of your family Gracie couldn't provide?"

"I do not," he said firmly, "have you confused with Gracie."

Perhaps he didn't; she didn't know. The theatrics and the reality were hopelessly entangled and winding tighter.

"I think we should slow down," she said gravely, "until we're sure what we're doing."

"*I'm* sure," he said, tipping her backward in his arms and placing her on the mattress. "And I'm not going to leave room in your mind—or your body—for doubt." He reached under her and unzipped her skirt.

She pushed ineffectually at his hands. "Your trip will give us time apart to think."

"That's right." He pulled her skirt and slip off. "But I'm going to think about you," he said, curling his fingers into the waistband of her panties and hose. "And I'm going to make sure you think about me."

In less than a moment he made it impossible for her to think at all.

Chapter Ten

"No." Joe smiled at Barbara as he shouldered his backpack.

"You don't want to come with us to the airport?" she asked, mystified by the children's casual attitude about their father's impending trip.

In a rare show of brotherly assistance, Joe held Jade's pack for her to slip into.

"Dad goes to the airport all the time," Jade said. "And the day camp's going to OMSI today."

Of course. The Oregon Museum of Science and Industry. No child would want to miss such an adventure.

Joe studied Barbara a moment, then put a comforting arm around her shoulders. "You know Dad always comes back, Mom. And he brings presents every time. We should send him away more often."

John, who'd just come in from the veranda with the paper, swatted him with it.

Joe laughed and reached up for his hug. "Have a good trip, Dad. You think you'll have time to look for Captain Kidd's gold? It's supposed to be buried in

Rhode Island somewhere, according to the treasure book you bought me."

"Jamestown," Jade informed him.

John shook his head regretfully and leaned down to wrap Jade in a bear hug. "Sorry. I'll be pretty busy in Warren. Take good care of Mom for me."

"Don't we always?" Joe smiled, pleased with himself and his continued performance. He seemed never to miss a cue.

Barbara saw John fight the smile. "Yes, you do. Promise me you won't take her to any bike shops and make her test-drive an ATV."

Joe pretended indignation. "You think I'd do something like that behind your back?"

"In a minute."

Joe turned to Barbara with a sigh. "Don't you hate it when he reads your mind?"

Her nod was sincere. "Every time. You guys have fun. I'll see you this afternoon."

Jade looped her arms around Barbara's neck and hugged. She wasn't the consummate actor her brother was. Barbara knew the gesture was sincere. She held the child an extra moment.

"Have a good day, darling."

Jade whispered in her ear, "Ask Daddy again if I can get my ears pierced."

Barbara caught John's curious glance. "I will," she promised Jade. "Don't wander away from the group at the museum, and stay with your brother."

Jade looked at Joe with a grimace. "I wanted to have fun."

"Now, be nice," Barbara scolded quietly.

"Yeah." Joe led the way to the door, Jade following.

"I'm nice to you."

"When?" Jade demanded.

"Did I let the zoo keep you when they thought you were funny-looking enough to put in a cage? No. I told them you were my precious sister and I— Oof!" His voice and what sounded like a fist hitting flesh were cut off abruptly as the front door closed behind them.

The adults around the table, even Joanna, laughed. Father Mike shook his head at John. "I don't know if that boy's going to become president of the United States or end up in some prison."

John groaned. "I know. Barbara and I have opened an account for bail money just in case."

JOHN SAW genuine distress in Barbara's eyes as he stood at the boarding gate and kissed her goodbye. Father Mike and Joanna looked on while Hal moved around them, taking pictures.

"I'll call you every day and be home for dinner Thursday night," John said, holding her. "You could pack for us so that we can start for my folks' early Friday morning. You know where I'll be," he reminded, "so call me if you want to."

"Okay."

She forced a smile, surprised that a lump had risen in her throat. What was wrong with her? The man was going to be gone for three days. Certainly she could deal with that without becoming emotional. But it was difficult. He'd become so important in her life. And the lovemaking that had caused them to be late to breakfast made her miss him already.

Then she remembered her promise to Jade.

"I told Jade I'd ask you again about having her ears pierced," she said.

The attendant called for final boarding.

"You think it's all right?" he asked.

"Well . . . yes," she replied. "I don't think it would do her any harm, and it might boost her feminine image of herself." She lowered her voice and added for his ears alone, "But she's not my daughter." That sounded like an untruth, somehow. Joe and Jade had become as important to her as their father. "At least, not really."

She walked him to the ramp as the attendant called his name.

"Well, she's going to be," he said, "so do what you think is best."

"John—"

He stopped to give her one quick and final kiss and a warm smile. "I'll trust you to do what's best for my daughter, if you'll trust me to be a great husband."

She knew how he loved his children and knew he didn't give his trust lightly where they were concerned. She didn't see how she could withhold her own.

"Deal," she said. Then she blew him a kiss as the attendant said his name with a new tone of desperation. "Go, before you're forced to chase the plane. See you Thursday."

She felt the world close up when he disappeared from sight and told herself sternly that she was being a ninny. She was a competent woman who'd gotten along just fine on her own since she'd gone away to college, and there was no reason she wouldn't be just as fine until he returned.

And she was. She took her entourage with their sympathetic glances out to lunch, then they returned to the office where everyone down to the mailboy was careful to call her Mrs. Cheney.

Hal took Father Mike and Joanna off to the photo lab, and Barbara settled into John's office with her garbanzo folder, determined to come up with an idea. But she didn't. All she did was stare at her cross outs and scribbles and think about John.

The children didn't seem to notice particularly their father's absence, except that they ran to the phone when it rang and remained near her every moment they were home. She couldn't decide if they were fulfilling their promise to John to take care of her, or hoping to find in her that edge of security that seemed to be missing in his absence.

Too wound up to sleep the second night because she'd dealt successfully with a client for whom copy had been promised but not delivered, she pulled John's robe on over her nightshirt and wandered into the kitchen. His citrusy fragrance clung to it and made her feel less lonely.

The children and Father Mike were asleep, and Hal had accompanied Joanna back to the manse because of a plumbing emergency. The house was strangely silent.

Barbara had missed John's phone call to the office, and felt both enervated and depressed. She thought a cup of tea and half an hour of raccoon watching might help her sleep.

Then she heard humming from the open door beyond the kitchen that led to Libby's two rooms, and went to investigate. She found the housekeeper polishing a shiny red and silver helmet with a screaming eagle on it. It seemed so completely at odds with the flowered wallpaper, the quilted bedspread and the chenille robe she wore.

Barbara stopped in the doorway and smiled. "Getting ready to ride your own bike again?"

Libby's eyes glowed. "Yes. These have served as flowerpots long enough." She indicated the second helmet that had yet to be polished. A perky philodendron stood in it. "I sold the bikes when my husband died because it all seemed too scary to me on my own. But Mr. Cheney's offer of the bike made me realize that you can be afraid, or you can be alive, but it's hard to be both simultaneously." She winked at Barbara. "At least, if you want to have any fun or accomplish anything. So I'm going to our family reunion next month, and I'm going to let my son-in-law introduce me to a retired highway patrolman he's wanted to fix me up with for the past six months. Romance is in the air. You and Mr. Cheney have inspired me."

"We're acting, Libby," Barbara reminded her.

Libby looked up from her task, met her gaze with a quietly direct blue stare, let it slip to the oversize robe she wore, then went back to polishing. "Acting like you're in love?" she asked. "Or acting like you aren't?"

Damned if I know, Barbara thought. It was becoming difficult to keep track of the situation.

She took a course parallel to the question. "I'm going to make tea," she said. "Want some?"

"Just made myself a cup. If I'd known you were up—"

"That's all right. I need something to do. Can I have a ride when your Harley comes?"

"First thing."

The ring of the telephone competed with the shrill whistle of the kettle a few moments later. Barbara felt her heartbeat accelerate as she picked up the portable, certain it was John. "Hello?"

"Barbara." His deep voice melted over her, warm and soothing. "My calls kept missing you today."

"I'm sorry," she said. "I was busy being Wonder Woman."

"So Hal told me. You actually got a team together and wrote the copy for the spot—and convinced him it was good—in an afternoon?"

"It's the kryptonite." She laughed. "It keeps me running."

"That was the Man of Steel not Wonder Woman." His voice had softened and she heard his smile.

"They were lovers, I'm sure," she said, moving to sit at the table with her mug of tea. "I've thought so since I was ten."

"You're supposed to have a magic belt or something."

"Bracelet," she corrected. "How is everything going in Rhode Island?"

John leaned back in the conference room chair and propped his feet up on the long table now empty of everyone but him. "Lonely," he admitted, picturing her in his mind in the middle of his bed. He'd longed for her since he'd looked into her eyes at the airport and knew she already missed him. "I never got lonely until you. I missed the kids, of course, but that's not the same."

She was dissolving into a puddle of emotional and physical need. She tried to think of something perky to say, but what came out in a husky, desperate little voice was "I miss you, too."

John let the words wash over him like balm. "Are you in the bedroom?" he asked.

"No, the kitchen. At the table, drinking tea."

"What are you wearing?"

Understanding that he was creating a mental image of her, she smiled as she replied, "Your robe over my nightgown. I cut quite a dashing figure, I assure you."

"*My* robe?" he asked softly. "Shall I speculate why you're wearing it?"

"No," she said, taking her tea and moving into the dark living room, knowing Libby's door remained open. "I'll tell you why." Safe in a big chair in a shadowy corner, she indulged herself, coaxed by his voice and by the aching hunger for him it aroused in her. "Because the scent of your after-shave clings to it, and having it against my skin makes me feel as though you're in it and your arms are around me."

"Barbara." His whisper was husky and low, but she heard it clearly. "In my heart they are. My arms are tightening around you and I'm pressing you close."

He bridged the distance of a continent, and Barbara felt him, corded muscles contracting around her until she truly believed she sat in his lap in the chair.

John heard her hungry sigh, closed his eyes and felt it against his throat. "Only forty-eight hours," he said, his voice weighted with desire and frustration, "and I'll be there."

The conference room door opened, and a dozen men dressed casually for a long night of business streamed around the table. More reluctantly than he'd ever done anything, John lowered his feet to the floor and prepared to tell Barbara that he had to hang up.

"Remember that I love you," she said softly, hearing the buzz of conversation behind him. "And I'm waiting for you. Bye, darling."

"Barbara—"

"I know you can't say anything—"

"The hell I can't," he disputed. "I love you, too. Keep the middle of the bed warm." She heard distant male laughter, then the honeyed sound of his voice again. "Bye, Barbara."

"Bye, John."

Barbara hung up the telephone and heard the bridge that had connected her to John break apart in the sudden silence. She was alone, and he was three thousand miles away.

Loneliness washed over her again.

Then she also remembered the rich sound of his voice promising to be home, telling her to keep the bed warm, and suddenly she didn't feel quite so solitary.

She sat up in the chair and examined the feeling with wonder, trying to analyze the lightness she felt, the subtle feeling that she'd rid herself of a cumbersome weight.

She realized what it was. Reality. With John more than three thousand miles away, she'd felt his love for her as though she'd been in his arms. And she'd telegraphed her own feelings across the miles. Theirs was no staged affair. They were in love.

The light of truth went on, brightening her shadowy little corner of the living room.

"Mom?"

With the sound of Jade's voice she realized that it was no mystical light, but the simple application of fingertip to light switch. Jade stood in the doorway to the living room in a faded green, Princess Jasmine nightshirt. She rubbed her eyes, a spike of hair standing up on the back of her head.

It had worried Barbara for several days that the children called her Mom so easily. Tonight her concern seemed to recede.

"Was that Daddy?" Jade asked sleepily.

"Yes." Barbara opened her arms to her, and Jade curled into her lap without a second thought, gangly legs hanging down. "He's anxious to come home."

"I know. When I talked to him this afternoon, I told him we're having my ears pierced tomorrow." Jade sighed contentedly, then giggled. "He said not to let them do my nose by mistake."

Barbara laughed, too, knowing she'd live the next two days for the moment he walked in the door.

"You're going to like Grandma and Grandpa," Jade said. "Daddy told them all about everything, and they said they can be pretty good actors, too."

"That's lucky," Barbara said with more enthusiasm than she felt. What would two fine, upright citizens think of the woman found almost naked in their son's office washroom? And if they were able to accept how that had come about, what would they think of her willingness to pretend to be John's wife, stepmother to his children and to share his room and eventually his bed?

It occurred to her that he may have spared them that detail, but certainly the rest of her activities were suspect enough that they would wonder what kind of creature their son had taken up with.

"We're going to have a clambake," Jade said, her voice fading, "and we're going to have to help Aunt Sandy decorate the church hall. Fortieth anniversaries are very special."

Barbara stroked her hair. "Yes, they are."

"I didn't think I was going to like you," Jade admitted sleepily. "I didn't think good mothers were supposed to be pretty." She snuggled closer. The early-August night was warm, but the air-conditioned house was cool.

Barbara rubbed the child's bare arms. "You have a lot of ideas about mothers," she said quietly. "You sort of gave me my training."

Jade closed her eyes and smiled. "Most kids' mothers train *them*. Now the other kids are jealous of us."

"The kids at school?"

"Yeah. Uncle Hal gave us a picture of you to show them 'cause they didn't believe us. *Nobody* has a nice mom that looks like you."

Prudence would have required that she remind Jade that the situation was make-believe and temporary, but it truly didn't feel like it at the moment, and it didn't seem fair to bring the child back to reality when she was about to drift into dreams.

The front door burst open, jarring Barbara into sitting up. Jade had fallen asleep.

The sound of high heels, clattering into the hallway was followed by the closing of the front door and another, heavier tread.

"Joanna..." Hal's exasperated voice drifted out of the hallway toward Barbara, but he and Joanna were still out of sight.

"I was *not* shouting at the plumber." Joanna's voice followed Hal's, high and ragged with uncharacteristic temper. Barbara had seen her suspicious, tense and judgmental, but she'd never seen her angry.

"You're shouting now." Hal's voice was quiet and controlled.

"I am not! I'm speaking loudly enough so that you can hear me! I told you I didn't need you to come with me to the manse. I told you I didn't need your help! I told you I could deal with the plumber without your interference, and when he walked out, I told you I didn't want you to call him back! That I would call someone else! But what did you do? Everything I told you *not* to do!"

There was a long, pulsing silence. Then Hal's voice said, "You know, if you don't want to find yourself a lonely old lady, you'd better improve your attitude."

There was a sputter of indignation.

"The plumber was doing the best he could while standing in six inches of water. When he asked you to stay out of the kitchen, I'm sure his concern was for your safety and not that he didn't want to avail himself of your divinely inspired advice. The way I understand it, clergy are supposed to help people, not lord it over them. That's God's job."

"Don't tell me my job." Now there was flame and fury in her voice. "You're a heathen!"

"I'd be willing to let you convert me if you could prove to me that you know something I don't."

"Thank you, but I tried that once. It doesn't work. Good night, Mr. Roman."

"I thought God encouraged that seven-times-seven forgiveness thing!" Hal called after her as she ran up the stairs. A door slammed on the second floor.

Hal turned into the living room, stopping wearily, hands in his pockets. Then he saw Barbara and the sleeping child.

"I'm sorry," Barbara said with a sheepish smile, indicating Jade. "I was an unwilling but captive audience."

Hal came toward them slowly. "It's all right," he said. "I deserve to be publicly scorned and humiliated for falling for Reverend Dragon Lady."

"Hal," Barbara admonished gently.

He leaned down to scoop the child out of her arms and led the way to the stairs. "Father Mike tells me she fell in love with a two-bit criminal she met while counseling at a county jail. She married him, and he ran off two weeks later with most of the church treasury. She's embarrassed and bitter."

"Understandably," Barbara said softly as she followed him upstairs.

He placed Jade in the middle of her bed and stood aside while Barbara pulled up her blankets and tucked her in.

"Bitterness is never understandable," he said. "It's destructive. She needs to start over."

Barbara turned to him, her own newfound insight helping her see what he felt. She smiled and urged him out into the hall. "Haven't you ever heard of the 'catching more flies with honey' theory?"

He heaved a big sigh. "There's so much in this world for a clod to know. Scripture, platitudes..."

"You'd be perfect for her. But go gently. You've let her know you're no pushover, and that's fine. Now show her that you have a gentle, caring side that will never hurt her the way her husband hurt her."

He leaned against the wall, glancing toward the other end of the hall and Joanna's room. He shook his head, then raised a hand to rub the center of his brow. "The woman gives me a migraine. She judges everything and everyone so harshly."

"Wouldn't you, if the person you thought you loved wanted only your access to a large amount of money?"

"I guess so," he admitted after a moment. He straightened and kissed her cheek. "Thanks for listening."

"Anytime."

Barbara watched him walk away, a not very tall, sturdily built man miserable with love. She found herself smiling. Love, she thought, should come with assembly instructions.

She peered into Joe's room and found him fast asleep on his tummy, Walter on his back, Hillary draped over his head on the pillow. Her heart swelled with affection.

She closed the door and went back to her empty bed—missing John desperately, but not quite as lonely anymore.

JOHN FOUND BARBARA and his children sitting in the
middle of the front lawn on a red-and-white check-
ered tablecloth, apparently having a tea party. But he
didn't recognize the blue willow pot and cups.

Father Mike and Joanna were absent, but Hal knelt
a small distance away, shooting the event.

They ran to greet him with flattering enthusiasm,
literally pulling him out of the car and across the grass
to the picnic. Jade and Barbara hugged and kissed
him, Barbara's eyes looking into his and telling him
how much she'd missed him, how much she longed for
the moment they could be alone together.

Joe hugged him, then punched him in the arm.
"I'm glad you're here, Dad. These two are getting really girlie on me."

Hal framed the four of them with his camera as,
arms around each other, they sank to the tablecloth.
Hal looked grim, John thought. Before he could
speculate why, Jade scrambled to sit directly in front
of John and hold back the short sides of her hair.

"I'm losing the light," Hal lied, getting to his feet.
"See you guys at dinner."

"Notice anything different?" Jade asked, turning
her head from side to side.

Tiny little star-shaped earrings studded her ear-
lobes. Barbara had told him last night on the phone
that Jade had taken the piercing heroically and was
dutifully following some turning and cleaning regi-
men.

He cupped her face in his hand and had a startling
revelation of the woman she would become—a mi-
raculous combination of her mother's mouth, his eyes

and hair, and an air of competent femininity that reminded him of Barbara.

She had curled her hair again and put on a blue sundress and her Sunday shoes.

"I like your earrings," he said. "You look beautiful."

She threw her arms around him and hugged him fiercely. "Thanks for letting me do it, Daddy."

"You're welcome."

"Do you want some tea?"

"Ah . . . it's not that chamomile stuff, is it?"

"It's orange cinnamon. We got it from Barbara's when we went to get the teapot."

Jade poured and Barbara explained as she helped him pull his jacket off. "Jade thought a tea party would be a good way to celebrate her new look when you came home, but Libby told us you don't own a teapot. I did."

Joe leaned against him while munching on a peanut-butter cookie. "Do you believe choosing to own a teapot, and not having an ATV? I don't understand it."

"Women are an enigma," John assured him, accepting his tea from Jade.

"What's that?"

"A puzzle. If it's any comfort, there are presents in my briefcase."

"All *right!*" Both children ran for the car, Jade momentarily forgetting her new dignity as she pushed Joe out of the way to reach the door first.

John turned to Barbara with a look half questioning, half amused. "The earrings were going to improve her feminine image of herself, did you say?"

She nodded without apology and picked a cookie from the plate in the middle of the cloth. "Today's woman fights for what she wants. It's part of her feminine makeup."

His wolf's eyes, suddenly focused on hers, sharpened her attention.

"Are you willing to take up arms?" he asked softly as the children started back toward them at a run.

"Duel...after children's bedtime," she said quickly. "Bedroom. Be there."

Certain his heart was going to beat itself to pieces, John gave her a look that accepted the challenge. Then he concentrated on his children to avoid anticipation apoplexy.

Joe exclaimed over the model of a sleek sailboat, patterned after one of the many elegant boats that sailed at Newport. Jade squealed over a pair of small gold earrings in the shape of scallop shells and gave him another hug. Barbara opened her foil box and found a gold filigree bangle bracelet.

She looked up at him, her eyes bright with pleased surprise.

"Wonder Woman," he said, "should have a bracelet." He helped her with the clasp, then brought her fingers to his lips. "Thanks for taking care of things while I was gone."

"Grandma called," Jade said excitedly, squeezing between them to pour more tea. "She said everything's ready for us. And Aunt Sandy said to tell you she bought the tickets to Hawaii, and she doesn't think Grandma and Grandpa suspect anything. They just think we're having a party."

"Great," John said. "I can't believe we're really going to pull this off."

Joe made a scornful sound, then slurped inelegantly from his cup. "Why?" he asked. "When we've tricked everybody into believing Mom's Mom—even her."

Chapter Eleven

John was almost surprised to find Barbara sitting in the middle of the bed wearing nothing but her bracelet.

He'd been afraid that while he took care of last-minute phone calls after the children were in bed, she would recall Joe's remark about tricking everyone into believing Mom's Mom—even her, and her fear would be revived that they were playacting, confusing fantasy with reality. Or that she might have remembered that she hadn't wanted a husband who worked in advertising and traveled, and would forget to keep the appointment.

But she was there like an apparition, the contour of her body a graceful, ivory shape in the darkness.

She lowered one foot to the floor, presumably to come to him, but he stopped her.

"Please don't move," he said, overwhelmed with the sylphlike S curve of her body in the shadows, thinking that artists agonized to put beauty on canvas, or to sculpt it, and couldn't approach what nature created with an offhand genetic configuration—woman at her most perfect.

He sat before her, putting a hand to her face, afraid to believe what he'd read in her eyes this afternoon.

She put her fingers to his cheek and smiled. "I know," she whispered. "It just...came to me after I spoke to you on the phone Tuesday night. I love you because you're not like my father at all. You travel because you have to, not because you're running away. And when I heard your voice, I felt as though you were right here with me."

"I was," he said. "I will always be. This is where I belong."

"Yes." She pushed up the simple T-shirt he'd changed into after dinner and pulled it off him. He lay back as she unbuttoned and unzipped his shorts and swept them down his legs. She folded them and reached to place them over the chair, but he sat up, reached an arm around her waist and pulled her back to the bed.

She fell onto him with a little peal of laughter. "I thought you were being awfully docile."

"I've dreamed about you for three days and nights," he said, sitting her astride him, "awake and asleep. I'm not going to wait while you tidy up the bedroom."

"I dreamed of you all the time, too." She lay against him, delighting in the way his bone and muscle supported her softness and took it into the concavity of his stomach, the hollow between his ribs.

John felt the tight tips of her nipples against his chest, the downy gate of her femininity against his lower abdomen, inviting him inside.

He groaned softly. She moved tauntingly against him and slipped her body downward, offering just what he was afraid of rushing.

She dotted kisses down the center of his chest, making his already-eager body quake with wanting her. She hadn't even reached his navel when he caught her waist and raised her over him.

Her hands braced against his upper arms, Barbara took him inside her and closed around him like a morning glory enfolding the evening.

They moved together in the eternal rhythm, turning in time with the universe. Pleasure tightened their orbit until they reached a pulsing center of waiting, reaching, wanting—then fulfillment burst upon them like a cosmic explosion.

Hands laced together, they felt the flash between them, lighting their world.

"Are you all right?" he asked, holding her tightly to him. She was shaking. He pulled the blankets up over her.

"I think so," she said. "Isn't it a little scary that we have that kind of power? Did you feel it?"

He laughed softly. "I imagine Mars felt it." He pulled her down beside him and tucked the blanket over her shoulder. She relaxed against him, flinging a knee over his thigh. "This is as real as it gets."

She kissed his chest, then ran her fingertips lightly over him, loving the suedelike texture of his skin. Then she held up her wrist, dangling the bracelet so that he could see it. "Maybe it's magic."

He pulled her up closer so that he could reach her lips. "The bracelet isn't magic," he said. "The woman is."

Barbara kissed him again, then settled back on his shoulder.

"Jade said you explained everything to your parents," she said lazily after a while.

He kissed the top of her head. "Right."

"Did you tell them what's happened to us?"

"That we've fallen in love? Yes."

That wasn't what she'd meant, but it would do for now. She was suddenly very spent, and it seemed better to let tomorrow take care of itself. She hooked an arm around John's chest and went to sleep.

TOM AND EDIE CHENEY stood "on-stage" on the porch of their home like a pair of Broadway veterans, waiting for their cue. As John turned his Safari into their driveway, Barbara could see by their smiles that they were eager to become part of their son's "John married Barbara" production.

Tom Cheney was several inches shorter than his son, with a thick gray mustache that matched the little fringe of hair around his head, and a comfortable paunch.

Barbara pegged Edie Cheney as the obvious source of her son's good looks. She was tall and slender in white jeans, a chambray shirt knotted at her waist. Graying dark hair was caught back in a bun, around which she'd tied a red bandanna.

They hurried down the steps of the old beach house with its broad front porch and sea grass growing up to the steps. The sun was high and warm, and the coastal wind blew gently around them, perfumed with the fragrances of places beyond the horizon.

Edie opened her arms to her grandchildren with a warmth that was generous and genuine. Then she reached for Barbara. But Barbara saw her careful scrutiny in the few seconds before Edie took her into her arms.

"Hi, Mom," Barbara said, hugging her lightly, afraid not to embrace her, for the sake of appearances, but also afraid that too emphatic an embrace would offend her. She looked like a woman who chose her friends carefully.

"Barb," Edie said with a smile, keeping an arm around her as she reached for her son.

John came into her arms. "Hey, Mom," he said, enfolding her and Barbara in a bear hug. Then he said softly into her ear, "What do you think?"

"The priest'll be a piece of cake," she replied under her breath. "But the woman looks like a hard sell."

John pulled away and introduced their guests. As his mother greeted them, he moved to embrace his father, bringing Barbara with him.

"How's my favorite daughter-in-law?" Tom asked, kissing her cheek.

"Fine, Dad," Barbara replied, trying desperately not to sound as shy as she felt. "I've been looking forward to your famous clambake for days."

"I'm ready," he said. Then he added quietly to his son as Edie and Father Mike laughed over something, "Good going, Son. How's it all coming together?"

"So far, so good."

"And you?" Tom asked Barbara. "Are you holding up okay? This guy's always got a scheme."

Hal was embraced by both of John's parents as though he were an important part of their lives.

Barbara found herself wishing she were, too.

The children led the way inside as Edie followed with Joanna, Tom with Father Mike. Barbara tagged along, arm in arm with John and Hal.

"You're doing beautifully," John told her. "Just keep it up."

"I've decided," Barbara said, "what you can give me as a bonus for doing this. *My* heart's desire."

"What's that?"

"I want your father to adopt me."

JOHN HUNG THEIR CLOTHES in the small closet that had been his until he'd graduated from college. Barbara placed underwear, socks and foldables in the drawers of a mirrored maple dresser.

The wallpaper was a soft pattern of yellow roses on a vine, growing randomly around the room. John saw Barbara looking at it when he went back to the bed for another collection of hangers.

"When this was my room, the wallpaper was signal flags. I think they redecorated so I wouldn't be tempted to move back."

His task accomplished, John closed the closet door and fell onto the bed beside the suitcase they'd shared.

"My father can't adopt you," he announced, lying on his back and stretching both arms out.

"Why not?" Barbara slipped the empty suitcase under the bed.

John caught her arm and pulled her down beside him. "Because that would make us brother and sister. I think you should just settle for me."

She affected a stubborn look. "I like your father."

"My mother's tougher than she looks," he warned. "And she's very proprietary about her family."

"Then what makes you think she'll let me have you?"

"Two very good reasons. First, you're everything she's been trying to get me interested in for years, and second, she has nothing to say about it."

She hooked an arm around his neck and rested her head on his shoulder, a curious feeling overtaking her. She felt the warmth and happiness in this house, saw in Tom's and Edie's faces that they adored their son and his family and would do everything in their power to help him. But a nagging sense of foreboding tapped at her awareness.

She wondered if it was because she found it difficult to *pretend* to be a family in the presence of such a fine example of one.

She tried to share that thought with John, but she wasn't sure he understood.

"That doesn't make sense," he said flatly, "because the 'fine example of a family' that you're talking about *is* the family you're pretending to be a part of. Anyway, I thought we'd concluded that we've all stopped pretending."

Then he reached under her cropped top, unhooked her lacy bra and banished all suggestion that their relationship was anything but real.

JOHN'S SISTER, Sandy, and her husband, Kyle, arrived for dinner with a new baby girl and a lively two-year-old boy. Edie immediately went off to the kitchen with Kristin, the baby, followed by both the twins.

Tom brought out a pedal car for Sam, who pedaled in one door and out the other as though it was a well-established route.

Kyle, Barbara learned, owned a small construction company, and Sandy had met him when he'd gone to the bank to open an account. He was quiet and easy-going, a contrast to his vivacious wife. He managed to draw Joanna into conversation.

Hal spent the early part of the evening taking photographs. After dinner he played with Sam, patiently rolling a colorful rubber ball back and forth across the carpet.

By that time John had Kristin on his hip and was expertly refilling drinks while the baby clung to his arm. Barbara heard baby giggles when he disappeared into the kitchen. His competence with children was both touching and intimidating to a woman who'd had so little experience with them.

She passed a dish of foil-wrapped chocolate mints to her right and found herself looking into Joanna's grave profile. She was watching Hal and Sam laughing together and battling for the ball, now behind Tom's chair, amid gales of laughter.

Despite the seriousness of Joanna's expression, Barbara saw vulnerability in it, and she probed her mind for something to say that would reach her. Over the past few days she'd begun to avoid conversation with her because it usually led to criticism or condemnation of something or other.

But Joanna surprised her with a heartfelt sigh and a quiet revelation. "I used to want children."

For an instant Barbara was at a loss. That was the first personal thing Joanna had ever revealed about herself. With everyone's attention on Hal and Sam, she struggled to generate conversation.

"Don't you still?" she asked finally. "I mean, a woman in her early thirties is much too young to give up on the idea."

Joanna turned to face her, and Barbara had another glimpse into her character. She was just another woman, flattered for being taken for several years younger than she was. She even smiled. It made a world of difference in her face, Barbara saw. She looked approachable, pretty.

"I'll be thirty-eight in November." Then a small frown pinched away the smile. "I . . . I don't have the temperament for marriage. A strict childhood, a sheltered adolescence and most of my young adulthood spent in divinity school left me—" She parted her hands in a gesture of helplessness. "Well, I don't understand how the game is played. I'm too direct and honest, and . . . a bad experience has made me . . . distrustful of men."

"Hal's as worthy of trust as any man I know," Barbara said.

Joanna folded her arms and crossed her legs. "I'm not interested in Hal."

"I don't believe that for a minute," Barbara replied evenly, "and I'm sure you know he's interested in you."

"He doesn't even go to church."

"He'd never hurt a soul, and he's one of the kindest, fairest bosses I've ever worked for."

Joanna turned to her in confusion. "I thought *he* worked for *you*?"

Panic clutched at Barbara's throat, and she forced herself to be calm, to think. No harm had been done. It was a small slip that could be easily rectified. But the knowledge that she could blow the entire complicated scheme in a heartbeat unsettled her so completely that she stammered.

"I . . . he . . . well, I met John when I came to work for Cheney and Roman, and . . . ah . . . Hal was my boss."

"I see." Joanna seemed unaware of her confusion and accepted the explanation without question. She turned her attention back to the man and the little boy. "I think he tries deliberately to upset me," she said.

"Because you treat him as though he isn't worth your notice."

"Because *he*—" Joanna began defensively.

"I know. But that leads to a vicious circle. Isn't your job to convert the heathen and bring him to the light? I happen to know he's looking for direction in his life, for stability and . . . family."

Joanna turned to her again. "He is?"

"He is."

"Barbara, can I see you for a minute?"

Barbara looked up to find John standing over her, a look in his eyes she couldn't quite define. She felt trepidation. He'd overheard her conversation with Joanna.

He smiled questioningly at Joanna. "Would you mind holding Kristin for a few minutes? Sandy's in the kitchen with Mom, and Kyle got a call on his pager. But one of them should be back in a minute."

"Well, I don't...I'm not... Okay." Her attempt to refuse the baby was nipped by Kristin's excited gurgle and the extension of both arms to Joanna.

John took Barbara by the wrist and walked her off into the kitchen. Edie and Sandy, stirring some kind of seasoning into a giant bowl of popcorn, looked up in surprise.

"'Scuse us," John said. "We're going into the laundry room."

"The laundry room?" Barbara asked.

John kept pulling her through the kitchen and into a small dark room on the other side. "It's the only place to have privacy without going upstairs."

"Put the towels in the dryer while you're in there!" Edie shouted.

John flipped on the light and closed the door. A harsh fluorescent tube revealed the standard white washer and dryer, and a table that held a stack of folded laundry and several magazines. A collection of children's toys was under the table.

John lifted Barbara onto the dryer, braced his hands on either side of her hips and frowned into her eyes.

"You heard me put Joanna on to Hal, didn't you?" she asked guiltily.

He raised an eyebrow. "No."

She uttered a gasp and raised both hands in dismay. "Then you heard me almost slip, didn't you? Didn't you?"

He frowned. "No. God, what have you been up to?"

"Well, Joanna said how she was distrustful of men and I said that Hal was trustworthy, that he was the kindest, fairest boss. Then she said, 'I thought *he* worked for *you?*' And I thought, Oh, God!'' She mimicked the feeling with a strangling hand to her throat. ''So I—!''

''Whoa. Whoa!'' John pulled her hand down and held it in his, the other resting soothingly on her thigh. ''Start over and tell me slowly.''

Barbara drew a breath and recounted the first part of her conversation with Joanna.

John listened intently, then shrugged. ''It sounds like you covered yourself, and it was a very small slip. I don't think it was enough to worry about.''

''But it made me realize how easily it can happen,'' she said, placing her hands on his shoulders and fidgeting with the collar of his shirt. ''I mean, after being so careful, after the kids turning in stellar performances and getting your parents and your sister involved. I almost blew it with a careless—''

He put a hand over her mouth. ''Nothing happened,'' he said. ''Everything's fine. We'll just think of it as a reminder to all of us to be more careful.''

She sighed, unable to shake the on-the-edge feeling of how close she'd come to ruining everything. ''Okay.''

''Okay. And what was that about turning Joanna on to Hal?''

''Oh.'' She was happy to discard the thought of disaster in preference to considering the possibility that something could develop between Hal and Joanna. ''Remember I told you last night about the fight Hal and Joanna had?''

He nodded.

''Well, Hal was really depressed because he truly feels something for her, so I suggested he try to be kind and gentle with her, instead of reacting to—you know how she gets." Before he could nod or shake his head, she went on. "Well, tonight she said…" She told him about Joanna's revelation about children, her admission that she knew she was difficult, and, Barbara's suggestion that she remember her calling and help Hal find stability and direction in his life.

John frowned. "Is he looking for those things?"

"Isn't everyone?"

He hunched a shoulder. "I don't know. You seem to think it's important, but a lot of us like to kind of, you know, live a less structured life."

"Structure is important for children."

"Hal doesn't have children."

"Joanna would like to have them."

John had no idea where to go with that or how to win if he continued to argue with her. Not that winning was on his mind at the moment—about the argument, anyway.

Barbara asked in concern, "If you didn't hear me slip, and you didn't hear me encourage Joanna to work on Hal, then why did you drag me in here?"

He tucked a hand under each of her hips and pulled her toward him. She wrapped her legs around him and grinned with sudden understanding.

"It's been two or three hours since I've kissed you," he said, teasing at her lips with his.

"Barely one," she said, looping her arms around his neck. "You caught me in the pantry when your mother sent me for Sam's teething cookies."

"It seemed like three hours. So kiss me now."

It wasn't difficult to give the kiss everything she had. It rose out of her so eagerly—passion, generosity, real, unadulterated love.

John took with greedy urgency, then gave back in equal measure. He gave her all the fire that warmed him, the power that sustained him, the light that had brightened every little corner of his life since the day he'd found her in it.

Barbara felt a little stab of alarm she hid from John with a crushing embrace. There was such a thing as happiness so complete that it couldn't be, wasn't there? One heard about it in torch ballads and read about it in novels of misbegotten love.

This was like that—born of an accident, too good to be true. And the line between success and failure was razor thin and just as lethal.

John felt the desperation in her and wasn't sure what it meant. Unless it was the fear she'd obviously felt at having come so close to tipping her hand to Joanna with a careless remark.

He held her tightly, then pulled her away to look into her eyes. "Everything's going to be fine," he promised. "Joanna didn't notice anything, and if you've put her on to Hal, she'll have other things to think about. We're going to do this."

She smiled, more than ready to believe him. "Right."

"Now, you're going out there," he said gravely. "Tell them you think you're having a sudden attack of malaria and you need to lie down. As your attentive husband, I'll have to go check on you, and we can—"

She rolled her eyes. "Where would I have gotten malaria?"

"You worked on the tropical tanning oil ad copy, didn't you?"

She took his face in her hands and shook her head over the pitiful suggestion. "Do you think anyone will swallow that with your wolf eyes gleaming so wickedly?"

He stared at her, shamelessly intrigued. "Wolf eyes?"

"You have wolf eyes. No woman has ever told you that?"

"No. Well, maybe we could tell them that *I* was outside bringing in wood and was bitten by a wolf. Yes, that's good. And you, as my attentive wife—"

She shook her head. "You don't bring in wood in the summer, there probably isn't a wolf within hundreds of miles, and we're staying with the party until every last guest has retired and every last dish has been dried and put away."

"And you once accused me of being no fun."

There was a rap on the laundry room door. "Dad?" Joe's voice called, then added in tones of confusion, "Are you doing laundry now?"

John dropped his forehead on Barbara's shoulder. "I'd sell him to M.I.T., but I just know one day he's going to do something brilliant and I want to be around to live on his residuals. Yes!" he shouted toward the door. "I'm putting towels in the dryer for Grandma."

"We're choosing up teams for Balderdash," Joe said urgently. "Grandpa wants you on our team 'cause you lie better than anybody." There was an exaggerated whisper. "And he doesn't even mean the...you know—the thing with Mom."

With a groan John straightened, yanked the door open and pulled his son inside. "Don't talk about that out loud!" he warned.

"I was whispering," Joe said, lowering his voice to demonstrate.

"Joe, I heard it through the door."

"Well, only Grandma was around. I wanted Mom for our team, but I think it's gonna be one of those girls against the boys things. Are you coming?"

Joe lifted the washer lid as he spoke. Then he frowned at his father. "The towels are still in here. What're you doing, anyway?"

Then he looked from one to the other and grinned. "Oh. So, should I tell Grandpa you'll be a while or what?"

John grabbed him teasingly by the neckline of his Trailblazers T-shirt and pulled him to him, saying with mock ferocity, "You know I could trade you to gypsies for an ATV I could ride myself."

Joe, hanging dramatically from John's hand, grinned up at him. "You wouldn't do that."

"Oh, no?"

"Who'd set your digital watch when we change back to standard time?"

Barbara held back a guffaw with a hand over her mouth. Joe made the best of the moment with an innocent look that reminded her of the one John used on her to good advantage.

John's laughing gaze shifted to her. "I could make

you part of the trade and ask them to throw in a TV/VCR combination."

"Who'd program Monday-night football for—? Never mind." Joe stopped and lowered his eyes when John's gaze snapped back to him.

"Give it up, Dad," he recommended. "You need us both. Jade, however, is another story. With her gold earrings, we could get a good price for her."

Tom appeared in the doorway. "Are we going to do laundry," he asked, "or beat the women at Balderdash?"

Barbara leapt off the dryer and began to pull the towels out of the washer. John caught the wet laundry as she tossed it to him.

"Let's go! Let's go!" Tom prodded them like a coach, until everyone was gathered around the dining table and the game—except Hal and Joanna, who sat side by side on the sofa, holding sleeping children and discussing the turbulent situation in Moscow.

Barbara smiled across the table at John, happier than she recalled being in a long, long time.

Chapter Twelve

When Barbara awoke shortly after 9:00 a.m., it sounded as though all the activity was already outdoors. She found Sandy alone in the kitchen, putting beer in a cooler filled with ice. Raucous male laughter came through the screen door from the beach at the front of the house.

"Good morning," Sandy said, looking fresh in a mint green T-shirt and matching shorts.

"What's going on?" Barbara asked.

"They're getting the pit ready for the clambake." Sandy went to the coffeepot and poured a cup, handing it to her. "The digging is becoming some kind of male rite or something. They're all trying to outdo each other. Trust me. Tomorrow morning they'll all be in traction."

Barbara laughed and sipped her coffee.

"Don't tell me Mom's competing?"

"No, she's on the porch shucking corn. But Jade was outshining Joe when they sent me in for beer. Joanna's on the porch, wrapping potatoes in foil."

"Can I help you carry that?"

"Please."

Barbara took one handle of the cooler and followed Sandy onto the porch. Edie called a cheerful hello, and Joanna was...laughing!...at the antics going on near the pit. Hal now stood waist-deep in the hole, shoveling up damp sand.

The men, including Father Mike, were shirtless, that very action seeming to make them half a step lower on the evolutionary scale than they'd been around the dinner table the night before. Their hair was wet and sandy, their backs sweaty, their voices loud. Piled on the sand beside the pit was a mound of stones and a pile of seaweed.

Joe stood in the shallows, hunched over something in a tidepool.

"That'll do, Roman," John called to Hal from the rim of the pit. "Jade can finish that rocky corner you're having trouble with."

"Yeah!" the child called, scrawny in a neon-flowered bathing suit bottom and a T-shirt.

Hal leaned on his shovel and squinted up at John. The sun was already high in a sky so blue it almost hurt to look at it. "Come down here and say that."

John leapt gracefully into the hole, prepared to take the shovel from Hal. But that wasn't what he wanted. Hal tossed away the shovel and assumed a combative stance. "Come on. Two falls out of three."

John looked up at the men peering with interest into the pit. They hooted and hollered. John looked back at Hal.

"Hal. Buddy," he said with exaggerated amiability. "I must have a foot on you."

"You do," Hal said, puffing out his chest and strutting across the hole. His friends howled. "And right now it's in your mouth. Can you take me down or not?''

John folded his arms and studied him. "Hal, I'll hurt you, you know I will. Remember the time you called Nolan Ryan an old man? It took you three days to fight your way out of the Dumpster.''

"I've been going to the gym.''

"To pick up girls. You have to work out when you go there or it doesn't help. You're sure you want to do this?''

Hal opened his mouth to reply, but Sandy shouted, "Beer's here!''

The men around the pit immediately lost interest in the squabble and went to the cooler. Hal grinned at John. "We'll do it tomorrow. Two out of three. First thing.''

"Right." John scrambled out of the hole and reached for Hal. "But after we come back from Mass, so I can pray for you before I kill you.''

Barbara was in a state of mild shock. She'd never seen John like this, nor had she ever imagined that the man in a three-piece suit with negotiating skills the UN might have admired could look so downright earthy.

Grungy sex appeal usually did nothing for her. She appreciated elegance and style. But this was something else. An appeal that was simply basic and unrefined, and captivating to a woman who'd grown up safe and "serious," because of the danger it posed.

With an arm on Hal's shoulder, John headed for the cooler, then noticed her standing aside. He yanked a beer out of the ice, touched his sister's bare arm with the cold can and darted away when she raised her hand threateningly. Smiling broadly, he hooked an arm around Barbara's neck and walked her toward the water.

She tucked her thumb into the waistband of his shorts and leaned into him, so happy she felt she might burst. His shoulder was sandy against her cheek, and he smelled of salt and ocean and man.

He reached around her with the can to pop the top, then took a long swallow. "Good morning," he said, planting a kiss in her hair. "Want a sip?"

"Thanks. I've got a cup of coffee in the kitchen. I haven't had breakfast yet."

"Mom always has a stash of scones in the freezer. A minute in the microwave and they're great."

"Thanks. Everything okay this morning? No breaches in our security that you've noticed?"

He took another long swallow and shook his head. "No. You?"

"No. In fact, I don't want to alarm you, but Joanna was on the porch laughing when Sandy and I carried out the beer."

"That's the beach for you. Mellows out everyone who walks across the sand and is forced to slow down."

She smiled up at him, hearing a note in his voice she hadn't heard before. "*You're* not thinking of slowing down?"

"Maybe," he said, turning his strong profile to the horizon where sky and ocean met in glittering brilliance. He turned back to her, his eyes as burnished as precious coins. "We're getting married next week. Did I mention that?"

She stopped in the damp sand, her mouth agape. "No. You didn't."

He nodded, staring at the top of the can he held. "I've been thinking about it." He looked out at the horizon again. "We won't be lying to anyone any-more—most of all ourselves. The kids will be thrilled and I—" His eyes came back to hers, full of love and promise. "I'll have *my* heart's desire and do my best to fulfill yours. We'll do it when we get back to Port-land to make us quickly legal, then we'll come back here to do it with ceremony when there's time. So what do you say?"

The casual stance he affected, waiting for her reply, was difficult to maintain. He wanted to shake her and plead with her—tactics he wouldn't discount if she made it necessary.

But she didn't. She put both hands to his chest, then around his waist. "I say, 'I do!'" she replied, laugh-ing.

Nothing in his life had ever felt this good, this right, this perfect. He lifted her up against him and laughed with her, turning her in a circle as cool water lapped at his ankles and the receding tide pulled at him. Her bracelet bumped against his chin as she framed his face in her hands and lowered hers to kiss him.

He felt a new, indefinable something in her, that somehow made sense for all its lack of definition. Maybe that was trust, he thought, the acceptance of feelings that made rightness out of what reason might consider nonsense.

He kissed the swell of her breast against the neck of her tank top. "I love you, Barbara," he said.

She wrapped her arms around his neck and held, filled with feelings so strong she simply hadn't the words for them. Except the ones he'd used. "I love you, too. But that seems to say so little."

"Not to me it doesn't. To me it's everything."

John went back to help the men line the hole with stones and build a roaring fire in it. Sandy explained that it would be allowed to burn for several hours, then they would place seaweed in the bottom, cover that with chicken wire and add another layer of seaweed.

"Those aren't razor clams," Barbara said when a large potful of very small clams that had been soaked in brine was placed on the seaweed. Razor clams were long and slender and slightly curved, like the old-fashioned straight-edge from which they'd taken their name.

"They're littlenecks from New England," Sandy explained. "Dad has them flown in by the local fish market. They're much more tender."

Tom added potatoes and corn and a dozen chicken halves, then another layer of clams. A final layer of seaweed was placed over the top, and the pit was covered with a tarpaulin weighted down by stones.

"Isn't it exciting?" Jade asked, hunkering down between Barbara and Sandy near the pit. "I wonder if the Indians cooked this way?"

Sandy shrugged. "I'm not sure. But the colonists did."

Barbara put an arm around Jade. "I know what you mean. It's nice to know we can do things without fancy appliances and electricity, isn't it?"

Jade nodded, then grinned. "But I'd hate to have to give up your curling iron."

Barbara laughed, and the three went back into the house to help Edie with lunch, since the clambake wouldn't be ready until dinner.

THE SKY WAS INDIGO, the day at the very edge of dusk and slipping into night. Stars were visible, and a cool wind had risen, causing them all to run into the house for sweaters.

The leftover food had been taken in, and a pot of coffee brought out and settled on a grate, placed over a new fire in the pit.

John held Barbara and Jade in his right arm, with Joe leaning against his left side. He studied his mother and father, sitting back-to-back, humming to the strum of Kyle's guitar; Sandy, a hand on each baby asleep on either side of her, her loving eyes watching Kyle as he hummed; Father Mike, a little apart, staring at the stars and probably communing with God; and Joanna, with her mind undoubtedly on things very unsecular as she and Hal leaned tête-à-tête, whispering in the light of the fire.

He thought about gratitude. He was a lucky man. He'd thought he had everything when his world had been simply him and the children. Then he'd found Barbara and learned that there was more—and that it, too, could be his. He felt more complete at that moment than he'd ever felt in his life.

Barbara decided that everything was going to be just fine. Every reservation she'd held had been erased in the course of the clambake, the volleyball game, the long swim with John and the hour they'd stolen in the middle of the afternoon when the children had been asleep.

For the first and only time in her life, she'd bene-
fited from the wild, impulsive streak she'd inherited
from her father.

"Daddy?" Jade asked lazily.

John touched her hair with the hand that held Barbara to him. "What, baby?"

"Did you think this would ever happen?"

"The clambake?"

"No, this." She pointed an index finger along the
four of them. "Us. That we'd find a mom in your
bathroom at work?"

For a moment the danger of the question asked in
open company didn't even register with him. He was
busy thinking that he hadn't thought this could happen, that in his wildest dreams he hadn't imagined
himself this happy.

Then Joe reached across him to smack his sister's
arm and Barbara stiffened against him. His mother,
father and sister straightened slightly in alarm. Kyle
dropped a note, then picked up smoothly. "I forgot," Jade whispered, her eyes wide with guilt and
worry.

But Father Mike was still staring at the stars, and
Joanna seemed to have completely forgotten anyone
existed but Hal.

"It's all right," John said, and ruffled her hair
again. But the incident reminded him how impatient
he was growing with the whole deceit.

What had begun as a challenge, and as a way to get
to know Barbara, was now chafing his reality. His life
had become what he'd been pretending it was, and the
possibility of being found out, however remote it was,
threatened everything.

He couldn't wait to get Barbara back to Portland and marry her. If anything parted them now, he didn't know what he would do. She'd become far more important to him than a national advertising schedule. She'd become . . . his. Like Jade and Joe, she was part of the fabric of his being, and he would destroy anything that threatened to touch a single thread.

Barbara tilted her head back to look into his eyes. "What are you thinking?" she asked.

He told her, thinking she should know how rooted his feelings were.

She kissed his chin, her eyes fierce in the firelight, telling him her feelings ran as deep. That relaxed him, somehow.

"RED AND SILVER?" John looked up at the crepe paper streamers that Sandy and Barbara held from wall to wall. They stood on ladders on opposite sides of the church basement, awaiting his approval. He winced, wondering how to put it delicately. "It's a little . . . gaudy."

Retribution struck immediately in the form of a wrapped roll of streamers to his head.

Kyle, standing beside him, gave him a pitying look. "I thought you understood. When you have an opinion that differs from Sandy's, you keep it to yourself."

"Stupid me."

"We have to decorate with red," Sandy decreed from her perch, "because the fortieth wedding anniversary is ruby."

John amended his position. "It's stunning. I love it. But why didn't we just reserve a restaurant?"

Kyle yanked on him just in time to prevent his being struck by the second missile.

"Because Mom's worked with St. Bonaventure's Auxiliary for thirty-three years, and they wanted to do this for her. A few of the ladies even volunteered to take our children home after dinner and sit with them until we get home from the party. I explained all this months ago. But, does anyone ever listen to me?"

"No," Kyle said.

"No!" Sandy answered her own question, missing her husband's quietly spoken reply. "So I'm forced to explain things over and over." Tacking her end of the streamers in place, Sandy reached for a red honeycomb bell she'd placed on the ladder's pail rest and missed, knocking it to the floor. She looked down at her husband and her brother and pointed. "Would you get that for me?"

The men looked at each other and shook their heads.

She raised an eyebrow, apparently refusing to acknowledge mutiny. She pointed again. "The bell."

They looked at each other again and gave her the same wordless reply.

"Guys," Barbara said, still holding her end of the streamers against the wall, afraid to lose the drape they'd worked so hard to achieve. "My arm's about to fall off. Get the bell."

"Sorry," John said, folding his arms. "It's the principle of the thing."

"There are no principles involved with crepe paper."

"There are principles involved in men and women working together," he said patiently. "Like mutual respect and cooperation. So far we've experienced very little of that from the two of you. It's been 'set up the tables, carry in the chairs, get the centerpieces out of Kyle's truck.' And now it's 'get the bell.' And all that without a please, a thank-you or a cup of coffee." He heaved a loud, high-pitched, dramatic sigh. "We're not taking it anymore. Are we?"

He turned to Kyle for confirmation.

"Ah..."

John's gaze sharpened. "Are we?"

"No," Kyle agreed, clearing his throat. "Of course not."

Sandy gave Barbara a dry look. "I know what this is all about," she said. "It's because we wouldn't open the box of donuts until everything was done." To the men she added, "I told you we'd have coffee when we're finished."

"And we're telling you," Kyle said, moving to the foot of the ladder, "if you want the bell, come down and get it."

Barbara saw the electricity arc between them. They'd been like a pair of giddy teenagers all morning. She imagined it was a rare treat for them to be together, without babies, for three or four hours. Father Mike and Joanna had volunteered to baby-sit while Tom and Edie relaxed and prepared for their big evening. Hal was supposed to be along later to photograph the decorating.

"Kyle, hand me the bell," Sandy challenged.

Kyle rested his hands on his hips. "Come and get it."

Sandy made it to the fifth step from the bottom when Kyle caught her thigh and her waist and swung her off the ladder. She squealed and landed safely in his arms. She smiled complacently. "Wouldn't it have been easier to hand me the bell?"

He tilted her backward, holding her waist to him with a muscular arm as her head swung toward the floor. She screamed his name, laughed and threatened, to no avail.

"Say, 'We're breaking for coffee,'" he ordered, "'and the men get the first pick of the donuts.'"

"We're not finished!"

He dropped her another inch and she screamed again and capitulated. "We're breaking for coffee!"

"And the rest of it."

"The apple fritter is mine!" she insisted defiantly.

"Ah, 'scuse me," John said, getting down on his haunches beside her. "But I want the fritter."

"Over my dead body!"

John looked up at Kyle. "Go ahead and drop her."

"Oh, this is good," Hal said, winding his way toward them among the tables and chairs. He made an adjustment to his camera lens and focused. "This will make my fortune. This is the cover of *Sex and Sensitivity* if ever I saw it." He snapped the shutter and moved around.

"Hal Roman," Sandy threatened, torn between laughter and indignation, "if you dare take a—"

"Sandy, please. Don't distract me." He got down on his knees, turned sideways, leaned precariously on an elbow and focused on her red face. "Smile."

"It's a matter of principle," Kyle said, ignoring her as she pounded on his shin with a doubled fist. The shutter clicked.

"It's a matter of an apple fritter," John corrected.

"Not anymore."

Barbara, who'd been virtually ignored since the fracas began, came out of the hospitality room's kitchen with a cup of coffee in one hand and the apple fritter with a large bite missing from it in the other. "Let her up," she said.

Kyle swung Sandy to her feet, then held her with both his arms around her waist as she adjusted to being upright again. "I'm sorry I had to do that," he said, "but you were getting a little bossy."

John straightened, grim purpose in his eyes as he started toward Barbara. "That was my fritter," he said.

She shrugged a shoulder. "Now, it's mine."

He quickened his step. "That's where you're mistaken."

She turned with a scream and headed back toward the kitchen. Hal followed them, camera in hand.

"IT WAS SO GOOD OF YOU to give up your morning to make this place so beautiful," Edie said, her eyes dreamy with sentiment as she surveyed the room. A sea of snowy white table covers were decorated with silver candlesticks and red candles surrounded by dried rose petals. Across the room the streamers hung, beautifully draped, complete with bells. John, Barbara, Sandy and Kyle looked at one another and shared the joke. "What are children for?" John asked.

Hal took Tom and Edie aside to photograph them against a draped window. Edie wore a scarlet dress bright with sequins, and Tom wore a tux with a red cummerbund and red rose boutonniere.

"I want a dress just like that when we're married forty years," Barbara said.

John put an arm around her and watched his happy parents pose. His heart felt too big for his chest.

"By then, a few of the Paris designers will probably be clients of Cheney & Roman. Who would you like to dress you?"

"Actually, I think I'll stay with Kate Cunningham. This is one of hers." Barbara did a small pirouette in a simple but clingy dress in a shade of royal purple that pinked her skin and brought out the darkness of her eyes. The soft knit clung to every curve and flared out saucily a few inches above her knees.

Desire bored into John's middle like a fatal wound.

Then Barbara caught his arm and pointed to the door. "Guests. Come on, we're on."

"IT'S GOING PERFECTLY," Sandy said to Barbara. They stood together on the sidelines after dinner had been cleared, the tables folded away to make a space for dancing. Then she asked, as though needing reassurance, "Don't you think so?"

Barbara put an arm around her and squeezed. "I do. You've done a wonderful job of coordinating everything. And dinner was delicious. Those auxiliary ladies are worthy of the Cordon Bleu."

Sandy heaved a satisfied sigh. "I've been so worried about it. I wanted it to be special, because Mom and Dad are so special. Father Mike's blessing was beautiful."

"He's grown very fond of them in just a few days," Barbara said. "So have I. They've even loosened up Joanna."

Sandy grinned. "I think Hal's had a little something to do with that, too."

Barbara didn't doubt that for a moment. When the Cheneys had all left for Mass that morning, Hal had driven off with Joanna to her church services.

Sandy tugged Barbara out a side door into the parking lot. She leaned against a pillar that supported a covered walkway and said gravely, "The twins love you."

Barbara nodded. "I love them."

"They've never even seen their mother."

"John told me."

Sandy shifted her weight and hooked an arm around the pillar. "I think all three of them, the twins *and* John thought they were fine just as they were. Then this whole crazy thing happened, Johnny dragged you in, and suddenly they all realized that a successful, well-rounded family needs a wife and mother in it."

"That was lucky for me."

"You've helped Jade become a little girl, not just Joe's twin. Joe thinks you're the most wonderful mother a kid ever had, and John has a light in his eyes that went out when Gracie kept her promise and never did come to see her babies. We voted informally last night, after you and Johnny went to bed, and you're in."

Over the last few days Barbara had watched the efficient Edie and the funny but competent Sandy at work and had only one concern. "But I tend to act on impulse. Recklessness isn't a good trait in a mother, is it?"

Sandy laughed aloud. "It should be a requirement! It takes a love of danger to find the balance between keeping them safe and letting them explore." Then she smiled gently and led Barbara toward the door and the sounds of music and laughter. "Jade told me how the two of you fell in the water at the zoo. She thought it was the greatest thing that ever happened to her. According to her, nobody else's mom, except some lady named Goodyear—"

"Goodrich," Barbara corrected.

"—Goodrich, ever has fun with her kids, and doesn't yell at them when they get dirty or wet. Just relax and be Barbara. That's the best thing you can do for anybody."

"What are you two doing out here?" John asked as he stepped outside, followed by Kyle.

"Girl talk," Sandy said.

"Uh-oh." Kyle frowned at John in the wedge of light from the open door. "That means they're tearing us apart."

"Maybe they were saying something good."

"Get serious."

"Okay." John folded his arms and blocked the doorway. "What, precisely, were you talking about?"

Sandy went to Kyle and looped her arms around his neck. "I was telling Barb," she said, "how lucky I was to find you in this world full of yuppies and no-brainers. How you meet my every need, emotional and physical, and that when you're not standing me on my head, you're the best husband any woman ever had. Want to dance?"

Kyle swallowed and ran a splayed hand up and down her spine, his eyes devouring her. "That's not what comes to mind, no."

"It'll be a nice setup for later," Sandy said, nipping at his lip.

He expelled a breath. "Then let's do it."

John stepped aside to let them into the room, then braced a hand across the doorway when Barbara tried to follow.

"And what were *you* talking about?" he asked.

She smiled up at him and wondered if this was what it was like to crawl into an earthen den and see the wolf in the shadows. All that was clearly visible were eyes, bright and golden and watchful.

She put her hands to his face and pulled it down to her, opening her mouth to welcome him. His tongue dipped gently inside her with that confident possession that was always in his touch, his eyes, his kiss.

She drew away to nip along his jawline. "I told Sandy how much I love you and the children and that I'm determined to be the best thing that's ever happened to all of you."

She kissed him again and felt his passion ignite.

"Just one thing," she said.

He raised his head warily. "What?"

She grinned. "Next time you go for donuts, buy two apple fritters, or we'll fight to the finish over it every time."

He laughed wickedly, remembering how he'd chased her into the rose garden behind the hall that morning and kissed her into relinquishing half of the fritter. "That could be a good thing," he said.

THEY DROVE HOME with Tom and Edie in the back seat, still staring at their tickets to Hawaii.

Kyle and Sandy followed with Father Mike, Joanna and Hal.

Barbara leaned against John's shoulder, too happy to speak. She couldn't wait to get home, to get into their room, into their bed and into his arms.

John suddenly leaned slightly forward to peer through the darkness with a frown. "Who's that on the porch?" he asked.

"Where?" Tom and Edie leaned out the same window as John turned into the driveway, pulling all the way in to leave room for Kyle to park behind him.

Barbara straightened, only half-interested, sure it was probably someone who hadn't made it to the party leaving a gift.

Then the headlights of the car almost up against the porch picked out a male figure sitting halfway down the steps, a hand shielding his eyes from the blinding lights.

Barbara gasped, her heart leaping into her throat. Trevor!

Chapter Thirteen

"So, it's true!" Trevor walked down the porch steps like a king descending the steps beneath his throne.

Barbara stood in the middle of the walkway, thinking that she'd almost forgotten what he looked like and that she hadn't thought about him in days.

Then she began to wonder frantically what she could say or do to prevent imminent disaster. Tom and Edie were out of the car behind her, and behind them she heard everyone else come forward.

She wasn't sure if the impression was truly physical or simply psychological, but she felt them pressing closer to see and hear.

Then John walked around the front of the car and up the steps.

"Come inside, Wentworth," he said, taking Trevor's arm and turning him toward the house. "I'd like to talk to you."

Barbara thought for a moment that the ploy would work, that John would get him into the house before everyone followed, explain the situation, earn his sympathy and send him out the back door, never to be heard from again.

She should have realized that was a naive notion.

Trevor aimed a fist at John's face. John blocked it neatly and turned him, twisting Trevor's arm behind his back. Barbara saw Trevor's awkward movements, then looked into the bloodshot eyes directed at her and realized he was intoxicated.

Kyle leapt up the steps to help John with the intruder. "Who is this clown?"

The front door opened and two gray-haired women, one small and frail and the other tall and sturdy, frowned at Trevor. "He says his name is Wentworth, and that he's engaged to marry someone named Ryan, who's supposed to be at this address. We tried to tell him that there was no one here by that name, that everyone staying in this house is named Cheney, but he wouldn't listen. He insisted, so we told him he had to wait out on the porch."

"She," Trevor said, pointing his free hand at Barbara, "is Barbara Ryan. My fiancée!"

John tried to haul him up the stairs, but Father Mike stepped out of the group and moved toward him. "Wait, John. He's probably just confused. She's not Barbara Ryan, young man. Her name is Barbara Cheney. She's married to this man." He pointed to John. "John Cheney."

Trevor, unfortunately not drunk enough to have difficulty connecting information, studied Father Mike. "You're on the Cooperative Churches deal, aren't you?" he asked.

Father Mike frowned, looking puzzled. "Yes. But how do you know?"

"Because I went to Cheney & Roman on Friday, trying to find Barbara, and got the runaround from the staff.

"They said she was on vacation for a couple of weeks, but no one knew where. But a man named Barnett happened by and told me there was a whole scam going down about *Mrs.* Cheney, and if I wanted to know more about it, I should meet him there Sunday, so we could talk with no one around. He said he owed Barbara. So, I met him there at noon and he told me everything."

"Young man—" Father Mike tried to reason.

"Father," Trevor said, "unless these two were married in the last week—and I know you've been with them day and night during that time—they're not married. If you've watched them walk into the same bedroom together, they're what your people would call 'living in sin.' "

Barbara felt an arm come around her, and she looked into Edie's smile. "Let's all go inside and talk about this," she said, hooking her arm into Father Mike's as they passed him. "Come on, Father. We'll clear up everything inside."

"We?" he asked.

She nodded. "I'm afraid we're all conspirators in this. Come along. Come on, Joanna."

Dispersing everyone to chairs, and dispatching Sandy to put on a pot of coffee, Edie hugged the two ladies from her auxiliary who'd watched the children and denied entry to Trevor Wentworth. They seemed reluctant to leave, looking back into the living room with great interest and asking questions as Edie pushed them firmly out the door.

Barbara sat in a big, old, overstuffed chair, dealing with guilt, embarrassment, anger at Trevor and her own stupidity for once having been interested in a man who could delight in revenge, and the desperate wish that things could have turned out any way but this way.

It's divine intervention, she thought. They'd tricked the representatives from a group of churches. How else could it have ended? She considered her earlier thought that everything was ending so well and couldn't help the glint of dark humor that crossed her general despair. Her mother had been right after all.

Though John had started this, she'd gone along with it and fallen in love, so that her performance was that much more convincing. If anyone was to blame for the completeness of the fiasco, it was she.

John saw the look on Barbara's face and resisted the temptation to shove Trevor Wentworth through the bay window. Instead he took pleasure in pushing him into a corner of the sofa where one of his mother's friends had forgotten a knitting project, needle protruding handily from the work.

Trevor yelped satisfactorily. John yanked him up, again, removed the knitting to the coffee table and pushed him down again. His father, taking the chair that matched the sofa, sent him a silent look filled with approval and amusement.

John sat on the arm of Barbara's chair, trying to reassure her with his eyes. But her gaze met his briefly, told him she loved him, then slid away filled with guilt and remorse.

Briefly, without much adornment, he told everyone gathered in the living room what had happened.

He began with his appearance at the prayer breakfast that fateful morning and ended with assuming responsibility for bullying Barbara into cooperating.

"I told her she'd be fired if she didn't help me," he said. "I told her it was her fault and that she owed me. That's the only reason she did it."

"No, it's not," she corrected him. Her eyes met his, but with a cool resolve he wasn't used to seeing there. It unsettled him. "I did it because the night before, I'd worn a special dress to Trevor's awards dinner. He barely noticed it, and when he was given a trip to the Cayman Islands and chose to take his father, never once considering to take me, I realized we weren't after the same things. So I decided to take part in John's campaign for the cooperative."

"You're saying what you were after with Mr. Wentworth was a trip to the Cayman Islands?" Joanna asked, a vague edge to her voice. Barbara saw Hal, seated beside her, turn to look at her.

"No," Barbara replied. "I was looking for a husband. When I realized he'd take his father to such a romantic spot to go fishing, I saw that he wasn't thinking of me in terms of a permanent relationship."

"But I was!" Trevor insisted, the picture of affronted dignity. "I came home early from the Caymans to ask you to marry me."

"Fishing must have been bad," John said.

Barbara ignored both of them.

"Something about John touched the reckless streak my mother always warned me about," Barbara went on. "I wanted to be part of the scheme and see if we could carry it off. Not because I wanted to deceive anyone, but because Cheney & Roman is a good employer, and I wanted them to get ahead. The entire staff does."

"So, you're telling us you had noble reasons," Joanna challenged.

Barbara shook her head. "No, I'm telling you I had selfish reasons, and they were my own. John had nothing to do with my decision."

"He says he threatened you with dismissal," Father Mike reminded her.

"He didn't mean it. He demoted the man who gave Trevor this information, because he tried to take credit for work I'd done. He wouldn't have fired me. He's fair."

"He demoted Barnett," Trevor said, "because Barbara *told* him Barnett had stolen her idea."

Barbara turned to Trevor, anger rising in her like a cleansing force. "And you believed that? That I would take credit for someone else's work?"

"Of course! The slogan he wrote was for a charter boat service. What do women know about that? What do *you* know about that?"

"I researched it," she said coolly. "And I wrote it while he was at a Mariners' game the night before deadline."

"The point," Joanna said, "is that you were hired to portray—or rather to *be*—the quintessential American family with a grip on its spirituality and a foothold in the secular world. And you lied." The last was delivered like a verdict.

"Not for very long," John said. "I fell in love almost immediately. She followed soon after. We are the quintessential American family you describe—it just isn't completely official yet."

"Meanwhile, you've—" Joanna waved a hand in the direction of the stairs, indicating, Barbara was sure, the bedrooms.

"Yes," John replied without hesitation at the same moment that Hal groaned, "Joanna!"

Joanna turned to Hal, her cheeks pink, her eyes snapping with anger and something deeper that caused Hal to frown.

"Don't give me that righteous groan," she said, getting to her feet and pulling herself up until her shoulders were square and her indignation apparent. "I'm beginning to understand everything. You were part of it, too, weren't you?"

"What do you—?"

"Father Mike swallowed all of it right away, but I thought I detected something," Joanna said. "A shyness in the way Barbara looked at John when he wasn't watching, a subtle something in the way he looked at her—as though he wasn't entirely sure of her. Those didn't seem like the qualities of a loving husband and wife, intimately familiar with one another." She gave the pair an accusing once-over, then glowered at Hal, who stood beside her. "So, you were to provide the distraction, weren't you? Keep the suspicious one busy so that she doesn't notice she's being hustled."

Hal stared at her, grimness overtaking his puzzlement.

"I dragged Hal into this," John said to Joanna, "just like I dragged Barbara. And there was no plan to 'distract' you."

Joanna looked from one partner to the other, then settled on John. "I find that difficult to believe, particularly from you. If you'll excuse me, I'll say good-night. And I think it only fair to warn you that I'll be calling Daniel in the morning and telling him what we've learned."

Father Mike stood and called after her.

Joanna turned at the stairs. "Good night, Father. My mind is made up. Yours should be, too."

Everyone stared at everyone else. It was over. The elaborate charade had been shattered by Trevor's sudden and unexpectedly ardent turn of mind. Or bad fishing. Barbara wasn't sure.

At the sound of a slam upstairs, Tom rose from his chair, pulled Trevor to his feet and walked him to the front door. "I believe you've done what you came here to accomplish," he said. "You're no longer welcome here."

"But I—she—" The door closed on his stammered justification.

Sandy and Kyle went upstairs to claim their sleeping children. Hal, after a thorough study of the toe of his shoe, sent a dark gaze up the stairs, then followed it.

Sandy, holding Kristin, wrapped an arm around Barbara as they gathered at the door. "Remember what I told you," she said quietly. "This doesn't change that. Wentworth's always been very self-absorbed. He's no great loss, Barbara."

Sandy hugged John and kissed his cheek. "It's all right. You did the best you could in a difficult situation and it didn't work out. So what? Tomorrow IBM will be knocking at your door. And the important things you gained through this are still yours."

"Right." John kissed her forehead, then the baby's, and walked them out to their car.

Kyle grinned at him in the light from the porch. "If you get desperate, I can always use someone on my second crew."

John punched his shoulder. "Get out of here. We're leaving in the morning, so we'll be in touch." He closed the car door and waved as Kyle backed out of the drive.

In the living room, John found Father Mike on the sofa with Barbara. He heard puttering in the kitchen and guessed that his parents had made themselves scarce.

"When can I marry you two?" the priest asked as John settled beside Barbara.

Surprised by the question, John turned to Barbara. He didn't like the concern he saw in her eyes. He looked back at the priest. "We were planning on the middle of the week, soon as we have the health certificate and the license together."

"Good." Father Mike smiled from John to Barbara. "I know the world doesn't consider this much anymore, but nothing gives marriage the solid foundation as vowing before God that you'll love each other forever, and asking for His help to keep the promise. I know you think you already have it all." His smile broadened. "But wait. Just wait and see what His blessing will do for you. Well." He stood. "It seems the party's over, doesn't it? So I'll say goodnight."

"Father." John stopped him with a hand on his arm. "Thank you for understanding. The afternoon that the cooperative walked into my office and found

Barbara there, I didn't really know her yet, so I thought the most important thing in my life at that moment, was securing your account.''

The priest shrugged. "Once, in the seminary, I solicited help from a fellow student for a theology test—during the test.'' He smiled self-deprecatingly. "I'd studied hard, and I have the heart of a priest, but the brain of a mule. Anyway, I was discovered and invited to the theology master's office. He told me I'd be doing an extra tour of duty in the kitchens and that I would have to retake the test. Not because I'd sought help, he said, but because I'd sought help in the wrong place.'' He smiled again, cheerfully, this time. "See you in the morning.''

John ran a hand down his face, feeling as though he'd just been chastened by God, Himself.

Barbara stood beside him, and he took her in his arms.

"You okay?'' he asked gently.

"I don't know,'' she said. "I almost can't believe it's all over. I'm sorry.''

He shook her gently. "Don't be. The important part isn't. We're getting married this week.''

Barbara kept her reservations about that to herself. The evening had been too traumatic all around as it was.

John led the way into the kitchen in search of his parents. He found them sipping coffee in a corner, talking quietly.

"I'm sorry your anniversary celebration was spoiled,'' he said, wrapping his arms around Edie. Tom pulled Barbara into his.

"Don't be silly," Edie said. "It was a wonderful evening. We have tickets to Hawaii and enough money to live like royalty for a month." Then she pulled away to ask him seriously, "Could you use a loan?"

John laughed. "No, the business is in good shape—even if this doesn't work out. We were looking for the benefit to our image almost more than to our bank account.

"Can you guys gather up Kyle and Sandy and the kids and come up for a wedding in the middle of the week?"

Edie beamed. "Of course we can!"

There were more hugs, more assurances.

"Sometimes things that seem the worst turn out to be the best for us," Tom said philosophically. Then at John's raised eyebrow, he added with a grin, "Or some tripe like that. The important thing is you were honest in the crunch. That's all the world asks of a man."

JADE AND JOE were sitting on the foot of the bed when John and Barbara walked into the bedroom. They were wide-eyed and wary.

"We heard everything," Joe said.

Jade's lip quivered. "What's going to happen?"

John opened his mouth to reply and found that Barbara was taking charge. She sat between the children and gathered them close to her.

"We're going home in the morning," she said, "and we've probably lost the account, but your father and I are getting married during the week."

John leaned a hip on the dresser, pleased but surprised by her simple explanation. He'd thought he'd seen hesitation, second thought, in her eyes.

Joe, also, looked surprised, then he smiled broadly. "Excellent!" he said.

Jade, who never trusted as easily, asked carefully, "And you're staying?"

Joe rolled his eyes. "No, dummy. They're getting married, then Mom's leaving to go with that geeky guy." He turned to give Barbara an incredulous look. "How could you have liked somebody like that?"

Barbara ignored him, apparently concerned with Jade's insecurity with the situation. "I'm staying."

"Our other Mom," Jade insisted, "didn't even want to see us."

John straightened away from the dresser at that, a dark line between his eyes.

"Nobody told me," she explained. "I heard Aunt Sandy and Grandma talking about it once."

He opened his mouth to speak, ready with a long list of reassurances, but again Barbara forestalled him. She pulled the children closer and said in an easy manner, "There are people in the world who just don't relate to other people. They can be very nice and very interesting, but when you need them, they don't notice it because they spend most of their time thinking about and looking for what *they* need.

"My dad was like that."

Both children looked at her in amazement. John saw the strong bond already forged among them strengthened further.

"The trouble was, he stayed and tried to be a father but it really didn't work because there were other things he wanted to do more than that. Your mother knew she would be that kind of parent, so she didn't stay. She made room for someone else to come in who really wanted the job."

Jade smiled for the first time. "You."

"Right."

Her doubts disintegrated, Jade kissed Barbara, then her father and went off to bed. Joe did the same, then stopped at the door with a hand on the knob.

"It's going to be hard to sleep," he said.

"Don't tell me." John went to him. "Because you don't have an ATV to dream about."

Joe shook his head. "No. Because Uncle Hal and Mrs. Gordon are screaming at each other in the room next door."

John peered into the hall and, sure enough, the sound of loud, angry conversation filtered toward them. Then the door opened and Hal stormed out. There was the sound of feet pounding down the stairs and across the living room.

John decided grimly that his friend had it rough. It didn't seem to him as though loving Joanna Gordon held a lot of promise for a man.

John shooed Joe out the door. "Now you ought to be able to get some sleep."

Joe peered back around with a winning smile. "You know, an ATV to dream about was an excellent—"

John put a hand to Joe's shoulder and pushed until he could close the door.

Then he turned to find Barbara sitting moodily in the middle of the bed, wearing the same removed expression she'd worn before they'd found the children in their room. She looked pale now in the bright purple dress.

He approached the bed with caution. "What?" he asked.

She parted her lips to answer, then closed them again and shook her head. Then she raised both hands in a gesture of desperation. "I don't know. It's all so complicated."

He sat facing her, a foot braced on the floor. "I might be able to follow," he said, his voice dry, "if you go slowly."

She gave him a lethal look. "This is not the time for your brilliant adman wit. I don't know what to do here."

"Where?"

"Here," she replied impatiently. "In this relationship."

She was getting testy. He wasn't sure if that was an improvement over that removed look or a worsening of the circumstances.

"You just told my children what you were going to do," he said. "You told them you were marrying me."

She nodded, her gaze unfocused. "I had to. They need to know their world is secure."

He didn't care for the turn this was taking. He studied her, trying to find a thread of reason to pick up. He finally gave up.

"I don't understand," he admitted.

She focused on him as though he interfered with whatever else was being worked out in her mind. "I can't let them down. That would be devastating to them. Besides, I love them. I couldn't bear to be without them."

That was good—sort of.

"And I'm...incidental to that?"

She treated him to another exasperated look. "Of course not. I love you." Then the look softened, became a little desperate and slid away. "But I'm worried about us."

Now he was growing impatient. "I love you, you love me, together we love the children. What's to worry about?"

"I can't forget that this all came about because I let myself into your bathroom." She climbed off the bed and reached for the nightgown she'd tucked under her pillow. She didn't look at him. "And if this has a bad effect on Cheney & Roman, which it's bound to have, I'm afraid one day *you* won't be able to forget it, either."

"Oh, please." He stood and pulled at his tie, feeling suddenly as though it were the noose at the end of his rope. He'd had a rough evening, and he selfishly wanted to hear her confidence, not her doubts. "If you've run out of enthusiasm for this relationship, please don't blame it on me. I am not now nor have I ever been the kind of man who blames someone else for his predicament. I told Daniel you were my wife, and that's what precipitated this whole thing. In which, I might add, I've had a hell of a lot of fun."

"I should have refused. I should have foreseen—"

"Barbara." John yanked at the buttons of his shirt as she balled the nightgown in her hands. "I'm not asking you to be my conscience or my fortune-teller or my business-of-life consultant. I take my own chances.

If you want to gamble with me, fine. If you don't, I won't make you stay. I'm going to take a shower."

Women! he thought as he stood under the spray of lukewarm water. Even the good ones were enough to drive a man to desperate measures.

He stayed under the water until he felt some semblance of calm, then reached through the curtain for a towel to wrap around his waist. Then he yanked a hand towel off the rack and buffed his hair, now calm enough to realize it probably hadn't been wise to tell her he wouldn't make her stay. The way his luck was running... He stepped out and walked into the bedroom.

He knew instantly that she wasn't there. He stood still for a moment, feeling the serrated edge of bitter anguish and disillusion. He had to lean against the dresser and put a hand to the pain. It flowed out from his gut in waves, radiating to every corner of his being.

He'd claimed to be a man who assumed the blame for his mistakes, he thought, through the grinding blur. This is what he got for giving her a choice.

Then a quiet and very familiar feminine voice said, "I'm right behind you, Cheney."

He spun around, joy instantly dispersing the pain. She stood there in the nightie, arms folded over small breasts almost visible through vanilla lace. The joy was doused as temper erupted inside him like a fountain of flame.

"You *hid* from me?" he demanded in disbelief.

She stood her ground. "No. I went into the bathroom to talk to you just as you stepped out of the shower with a towel over your head and walked in here." She yanked at the towel that had slipped to his neck and took both ends in her hands.

"Don't you ever minimize my concerns," she said, "by telling me to get over them or get out."

He had to lean down to allow her control of the towel, yet the look in her eye was fascinating. This was a side of Barbara he hadn't seen before. It was a darker variation of the firm way she'd dealt with Jade and Joe's fears.

"I did not tell you to 'get out,'" he said, repeating those words with the scorn they deserved. "I told you I wouldn't make you stay."

"So I thought I'd let you see what your life would feel like without me."

She saw instantly that had not been a wise thing to say. He straightened, snapping the towel out of her hands. He yanked it off and tossed it aside. Then he swept her off her feet and carried her to the bed, his eyes dangerous. "Then maybe you'd like to feel what it's like to toy with a man's affections."

"I did not—" He dropped her in the middle of the pillows, and the single bounce terminated her denial.

"You did," he said, his expression without one betraying hint of humor. She felt a niggle of concern. "You stayed behind me as I walked into the room so that I would think you'd gone."

She sat up in a huff, determined to make him listen. "I wanted to get your attention," she said. "I wanted you to realize I'm important to you, to take me seriously when I tell you I'm a little worried that the way this all started may...make it hard to hold."

"You are important to me," he said angrily, "and do *you* listen to *me* when I tell you there's nothing to

worry about? That I'll love you into eternity whatever the hell happens to the business or to us? No."

Barbara found that she could not ignore such emphasis. He leaned over her, eyes blazing, shoulders
bare, and she accepted once and for all that he was
right. She'd seen his shoulders slump when he'd
thought she was gone, heard the low, strangled sound
in his throat as he leaned against the dresser. The picture had been clearer than a look at his face.

"Okay, okay," she said gently, planting a kiss on his
shoulder. "I'm sorry. The evening was kind of a shock
and I got a little panicky."

She undid the tuck in his towel and hitched a leg
over him.

John saw nothing after that but the wave of her hair
falling over his face and her lips coming at him. Then
she was atop him, containing him, and everything he
knew for certain fled his mind, except her love.

Chapter Fourteen

"Where's Hal?" John, packing the van to leave for home, took the bag his father handed him and tucked it into a corner. "Where's his bag?"

"He left after you and Barbara went to bed," Tom said, holding out empty hands. "That's the last of it."

John closed the tailgate and frowned at Tom. "What do you mean, he left? In what? We all rode together."

"A cab. Said he had things to do."

John would have closed his eyes and taken a moment to collect himself, but there wasn't time. Joanna had informed them at 8:00 a.m. that she'd spoken to Daniel Burger, and he and the other members of the cooperative would be meeting them at the office at noon. It was now after nine. If he was going to have time to drop the children at home, he had to hit the road.

He'd have preferred to have his friend and partner at his side when he faced the cooperative, but he understood Hal's anguish over Joanna. And Hal wasn't the one who'd gotten them into this; he was.

"All right," he called to the subdued little group exchanging hugs and handshakes in the driveway. "Let's go."

"It's going to be fine," Edie said as she held him to her when everyone else was in the car. "I feel it. Father Mike's on your side."

John shook his head. "Thanks, Mom, but the cooperative's decision on anything has to be unanimous, and they'd rather change plans than lose a member. I blew it."

"Hindsight's twenty-twenty," Tom said, giving him a bear hug. He had to admit it felt good. "Brave people look ahead."

John smiled at him as he pulled away. "You're full of philosophy lately."

Tom put an arm around Edie. "Comes from living with your mother. I find I have to get philosophical about a lot of things."

The drive home was eerily quiet. Father Mike played word games with the children, but Joanna sat alone in the middle seat, face set and hurt.

Late summer traffic was thick on the coast, and John found himself less patient than usual. He had to admit he was worried. The reputation of Cheney & Roman was on the line. Now that he and Barbara had settled things between them, he allowed himself to worry about the business.

When he stopped at a lineup of cars waiting to merge off a beachfront road to the highway, Barbara leaned sideways in her seat and reached out to turn his face to her. She kissed him gently. "I love you," she said.

He felt something relax inside him. He was grateful that, at least, was settled.

THE CHILDREN BOLTED from the van at the sight of a helmeted figure on a motorcycle, circling the front lawn. He had to take a moment to watch and smile.

"Libby's Harley came!" Barbara exclaimed, leaning over him to peer out the window as the bike turned in their direction, the children following. Then Barbara sobered and looked into his eyes. "But the deal . . ."

John shook his head. "She did her part. Life's too short to belabor the fine print. Here I thought I had everything, then I found you, and now I probably only have fifty years to enjoy you. I should have looked for you sooner."

Barbara kissed him soundly. "I'll make the fifty years so great you won't think anything's missing— even time."

"Hi! Welcome home!" The visor on the helmet went up and Libby's face beamed at them. "It came this morning!" she shouted, probably still hearing the roar in her ears. She reached in to hug her employer, bumped her helmet on the roof of the Safari, then laughed as she pulled it off. She reached in again and gave him a resounding kiss on his cheek. "Thank you!" she gushed. "I've had the best morning!"

Father Mike hung out the side window, crowding a grumpy Joanna to the other seat.

Libby waved at him, then frowned at John. "But your mom called and said—" She spotted Joanna in the middle seat and stopped.

"It isn't over yet," John said. "And anyway, the bike's yours. Just keep the kids off it, okay? We should be home for dinner."

"Right." She walked the bike backward like a veteran of the road. "Good luck!"

CAROL MET THEM at the elevator and dispatched another secretary to take Father Mike and Joanna to the conference room. She held John and Barbara back and walked slowly between them toward the big double doors.

"We held our own staff meeting this morning," she said softly as watchful eyes looked up from scores of desks and offered encouragement. "And we want you to know you have our vote as the best ad team in the business, whether or not the cooperative gives you theirs." She stopped at the doors and added with a hand on her hip, "Unless losing this account results in a loss of revenue and a dip in salaries. Then we're all out of here."

John gave her a hug. "What a devoted crew."

"Good luck," she whispered.

John pulled the doors open and stepped into the room before Barbara, ready to protect her an extra moment against the assault of the cooperative's disapproval. But they were all crowded at the end of the table, poring over something he couldn't see. Daniel sat at the head of the table, and Hal leaned over him, pointing.

Only Joanna stood aside, her arms folded, her lips pursed.

Barbara physically pushed John out of her way and stood beside him. "What's going on?" she whispered. "What are they looking at?"

"Gallows plans?" he guessed. Then he walked into the room. "Good afternoon, gentlemen."

"John." Daniel looked up from the table, an indeterminate look on his face. He was without his customary smile. Then he flashed it briefly. "Barbara. Come and join us."

John approached the table and saw photographs, some taken as recently as the day before. Hal must have been up all night developing them. John looked up at his partner for an explanation.

Hal shrugged a shoulder. "I couldn't sleep so I came home early to have at least part of a presentation ready."

John walked around Daniel's chair to study the shot he was inspecting so closely. It was one of the group taken at the airport when Barbara had seen him off to Rhode Island. Love brimmed in her eyes and shone blatantly in his.

Daniel picked up several more. One was of Barbara and Jade, balanced like ballerinas on the wall surrounding the zoo's duck pond. In the next they were wet as a pair of seals as they surfaced, looking at each other and laughing. There was a third of him, trying desperately to look severe and failing, as he hauled them out.

"If we were going to do this," Daniel said, selecting another photo he'd placed at hand, "this would be the centerpiece. It says everything."

Barbara went around to look. It was a photograph taken the night before at his parents' party. They were slightly out of focus in the background, looking toward him and Barbara, who were standing on opposite sides of the children. Jade and Joe were in an animated conversation, and he and Barbara were simply smiling at each other, he in his suit, she in her slim purple dress.

They weren't touching, except with their eyes. That indefinable something that binds man and woman for a lifetime was as clear between them as if it had physical substance.

Barbara's arm stole around his waist. John wrapped an arm around her shoulders and looked up at Hal, a catch in his throat. His friend looked both proud and miserable.

"Sit down, please," Daniel said briskly, gesturing toward chairs. "We have to decide what to do here. The cooperative must vote."

John led Barbara to a chair. This was simply a formality, he knew. He'd heard that remark, "If we were going to do this," the choice of words suggesting he'd decided not to.

Barbara cleared her throat and took her courage in her hands. "Reverend Burger, I know Joanna told you that we tricked you, and we don't deny it, but I think you should hear our—"

Daniel silenced her with a look. "I had a telephone call this morning from John's mother and another from John's sister, filling me in on 'the other side.'" His voice emphasized the words. He smiled thinly. "I was also stopped first thing this morning by John's secretary, who was chosen as spokesman for your staff. She regaled me for twenty minutes with a litany of your virtues, John, and Cheney & Roman's refusal to take alcohol or tobacco clients, their improved health-care policy for employees, profit sharing, fully equipped gymnasium."

"The point," Joanna said, taking a chair at the end of the group, "is that they lied to us and misrepresented all the qualities we were hoping to tap with this campaign."

"The point," Hal said, taking the chair opposite her, "is that your hurt feelings, your belief in your own fabrication, and your inability to loosen up because you can't forgive yourself for one mistake, are coloring your judgment, Joanna."

"Hal," John said quietly.

Hal ignored him. "You told me the night of the clambake that you regretted doubting them in the beginning, that the beach had given you a new perspective on everything."

"We've been deceived," Joanna said to Daniel.

Daniel nodded. "I believe there's been a deception here, all right."

Barbara took John's hand under the table, squaring her shoulders.

"But I believe *we* were not the victims of it," Daniel went on. He held up the photo taken at the anniversary party. "John told us—or, rather, I believe I assumed—that he and Barbara were passionately in love. Is there anything in this photo that would cause you to doubt the truth of that?"

Members of the cooperative looked at one another. Joanna tried to speak, but Daniel interrupted her. Hal smiled at John and Barbara.

"Joanna tells us they weren't married when we walked in on them that afternoon. I've explained to you what Edie Cheney and Sandy Ryder told me about the incident. John wanted our account and did his best to save the day.

"I believe the most obvious deceit here was between these two when they told themselves they were acting. Does that look like acting?" He held up the airport photo.

Barbara turned to John, who squeezed her hand but remained calm, listening.

Daniel turned to Joanna, studied her for a moment with a smile Barbara thought was almost apologetic. She had only a moment to wonder what it meant. Daniel picked up another photo and passed it down to her.

"And my companions and I are victims of another deception, Joanna, if you want us to believe that you haven't fallen in love yourself—with the man who took that photograph."

Barbara strained to see as the photo was passed to Joanna. In it, she sat in the shallows in a pair of John's mother's cutoffs, her calves and feet bare, her short hair ruffled, her smile wide and free—and all for the man shooting the picture. Hal.

Joanna tried to push away from the table, but Hal was around it and behind her, blocking her in place with his arms on either side of her. "You have to vote before you leave," he said.

"I ask you to do what you believe to be best," Daniel said. "Our votes are required to be unanimous, but we have high hopes for this project, and we want everyone to believe in it, if we proceed."

Daniel began to poll. There were five out of six ayes when the vote reached Joanna.

"Can you fault them for falling in love," Hal asked softly, "when you fell in love yourself?"

Joanna held herself stiffly away from him. "That was before I knew you'd used me."

"I didn't use you," Hal insisted gently, sincerely. "I fell in love with you."

"Hal," John said quietly, "I don't think you can influence a vote like that and expect it to have any binding—"

"This whole thing is about truth, isn't it?" Hal said, unmoved by John's mild censure. "Aren't we searching for the truth, Joanna? Do you love me, or not?"

"The truth," Barbara said to Joanna, "is that Hal was already in love with you the night the manse's plumbing burst. He asked me for àdvice after your quarrel that night. I'm the one who suggested he get to know you better, try to learn what you needed. It was no trick."

Joanna turned slightly in her chair to look over her shoulder at Hal. Her eyes were wide and suspicious and spilling tears.

Hal pulled her out of her chair and into his arms. "I love you, Joanna. I declare it in front of the cooperative of churches and my business partners. Would a lying man do that?"

Daniel asked calmly, "Your vote, Joanna?"

"Yes!" she cried, turning to sob into Hal's shoulder. "Yes!"

There was a shriek beyond the double doors, followed by the sound of a general commotion. Daniel looked at John.

"My secretary, I believe," John said.

"Well." Daniel and his group stood. Daniel shook John's hand, then Barbara's. "I believe this is going to be a happy association. Father Mike tells me he'll be marrying the two of you this week."

"That's right," John said. "You're invited to the wedding—all of you."

"We'll be there." He indicated Hal and Joanna, still holding each other and talking quietly. "We may have to schedule two."

While John and Barbara walked Daniel and the co-operative to the front doors, Carol sat sedately at her desk, and all heads were bent industriously over drafting tables and computer terminals.

The moment the doors closed, pandemonium broke loose. Barbara leapt into John's arms, triumphant shouts filled the room and papers and streamers flew in the air. Pizza and champagne were delivered, and the party lasted until dinner.

Hal and Joanna had already left, arm in arm, smiles blinding, when John fell into the chair behind his desk and pulled Barbara into his lap.

"Do you believe this happened?" he asked her lazily.

"Yes," she replied, leaning her head on his shoulder. "It was a miracle, but these people deal in miracles. That's their business. We're going to have to get used to that if they're going to be our clients. And used to it on a national level."

"It was Hal, loving Joanna," John said, holding Barbara close and thinking how completely her love affected him, inspired him, renewed him.

Barbara, who'd once sought to replace love with order and system, held fast to the man who'd changed her life. "That's what I just said," she told him. "Love is the miracle."

Epilogue

St. Bonaventure's was filled with flowers.

"I've never seen so many people," Edie said, peering from the vestibule into the body of the church, "at a wedding that was planned in five days!"

Barbara, in an ivory tea-length gown, thought that no one was more surprised than the bride herself. The pews were filled with many of John's friends, all the Cheney & Roman employees, many of their clients and Libby's family, who'd arrived the previous evening on motorcycles.

Barbara's mother was in the front pew, and her stepfather stood a few feet away talking to Tom and waiting to escort her up the aisle.

Her father had called from Tokyo to congratulate her, wish her well and tell her that a snag in the construction of the apartment complex he'd designed precluded his coming for the wedding.

She couldn't deny that part of her had hoped against hope that he would come to give her away. But another part of her looked around at her mother and stepfather, at Jade and Joe, the children who'd been hers almost from the moment she'd met them, at her

new in-laws and at John, the man who'd made her
dreams real, and could feel no disappointment. She
lacked nothing that was important to her.

Jade put her basket of rose petals aside and fluffed
the ruffled sleeves of Barbara's dress. "You look great,
Mom," she said. "Dad'll faint when he sees you."

Barbara smiled, having difficulty imagining John in
a faint. "You look beautiful, too," she said.

Jade picked up her basket and ran rose petals
through her fingers. She frowned up at Barbara. "You
know, it's weird that they let you litter in a church."

Carol and Sandy, Barbara's matron of honor and
bridesmaid in different shades of yellow, emerged
from the dressing room.

Carol smiled at Barbara's hat. "Your chapeau is
dynamite."

"The rose was my idea," Sandy said with no attempt at modesty.

Barbara touched the broad-brimmed hat, the front
pinned back to the crown with a champagne rose from
her bouquet. "Is it straight?"

"It's perfect."

"All right. Groom coming through." There was a
sudden commotion of protest as John and Joe forced
their way into the little cluster of women.

"John!" Edie said, trying to push him away. "It's
bad luck for you to see the bride before—"

"I know, I know." He fended her off gently. "But
it's an emergency."

"What?" the five women demanded in unison.

He flashed a disarming smile. "I missed her." He
took her hands and pulled her into a corner with the
children.

"Everything okay?" he asked, his eyes going over every beautiful detail of her glowing face, her soft shoulders, and the subtle swell of bosom disappearing into the ivory silk.

"Everything's wonderful," she said, thinking deep down how absolutely true that was. "But I'm glad you missed me."

He was breathtakingly handsome in a dark suit and a paisley bow tie that had been a gift from Hal and Joanna, who would be married the following week.

Joe, beside him, also wore a suit for his role as a groomsman. But the more formal clothing did not diminish the devilish glint in his eyes.

"Uncle Hal tried to tell him you were fine," he said, "but he had to see for himself. Now we're probably gonna have bad luck or something."

John, his eyes still looking into Barbara's, shook his head. "Not a chance. We're charmed. Or, I suppose Father Mike would call it 'blessed.'" He leaned forward to kiss her gently, careful of her hat. "We just came to tell you that we love you. And we're so grateful that you belong to us."

Jade, always cautious, reminded him, "You told me that we belong to each other."

He touched her hair in its coronet of yellow roses. "You're right."

Her heart full enough to burst, Barbara placed an arm around each of the children and leaned toward John.

He wrapped them all in his embrace, emotion crowding his throat.

"John!" Edie whispered. "Father's calling for you."

"Be right there." He gave Barbara one last look that said everything she would ever want to know about his love for her.

She squeezed his hand. "We are blessed," she whispered.

"John!" Edie's whisper was desperate.

Everyone scattered: John and Joe to run around to the side entrance to take their places at the altar with Hal; Edie and Tom to take their places; Carol, Sandy and Jade to line up at the door as the music began.

Barbara stood with her stepfather in the wide doorway as the women began the procession, and Jade followed, "littering" the carpeted aisle with rose petals.

The church seemed to burst with music, flowers, smiling faces waiting for her and the rampant joy of a happy wedding.

It was like a dream, she thought, starting up the aisle. But she couldn't imagine a dream that could compare with her reality.

MILLION DOLLAR SWEEPSTAKES (III)

No purchase necessary. To enter the sweepstakes and receive the Free Books and Surprise Gift, follow the directions published and complete and mail your "Win A Fortune" Game Card. If not taking advantage of the book and gift offer or if the "Win A Fortune" Game Card is missing, you may enter by hand-printing your name and address on a 3" X 5" card and mailing it (limit: one entry per envelope) via First Class Mail to: Million Dollar Sweepstakes (III) "Win A Fortune" Game, P.O. Box 1867, Buffalo, NY 14269-1867, or Million Dollar Sweepstakes (III) "Win A Fortune" Game, P.O. Box 609, Fort Erie, Ontario L2A 5X3. When your entry is received, you will be assigned sweepstakes numbers. To be eligible entries must be received no later than March 31, 1996. No liability is assumed for printing errors or lost, late or misdirected entries. Odds of winning are determined by the number of eligible entries distributed and received.

Sweepstakes open to residents of the U.S. (except Puerto Rico), Canada, Europe and Taiwan who are 18 years of age or older. All applicable laws and regulations apply. Sweepstakes offer void wherever prohibited by law. Values of all prizes are in U.S.currency. This sweepstakes is presented by Torstar Corp, its subsidiaries and affiliates, in conjunction with book, merchandise and/or product offerings. For a copy of the official rules governing this sweepstakes offer, send a self-addressed, stamped envelope (WA residents need not affix return postage) to: MILLION DOLLAR SWEEPSTAKES (III) Rules, P.O. Box 4573, Blair, NE 68009, USA.

SWP-H494

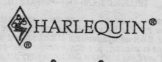

WEDDING INVITATION
Marisa Carroll

Brent Powell is marrying Jacqui Bertrand, and the whole town of Eternity is in on the plans. This is to be the first wedding orchestrated by the newly formed community co-op, Weddings, Inc., and no detail is being overlooked.

Except perhaps a couple of trivialities. The bride is no longer speaking to the groom, his mother is less than thrilled with her, and her kids want nothing to do with *him.*

WEDDING INVITATION, available in June from Superromance, is the first book in Harlequin's exciting new cross-line series, **WEDDINGS, INC.** Be sure to look for the second book, **EXPECTATIONS,** by Shannon Waverly (Harlequin Romance #3319), coming in July.

American Romance is goin' to the chapel...with three soon–to–be–wed couples. Only thing is, saying "I do" is the farthest thing from their minds!

You're cordially invited to join us for three months of veils and vows. Don't miss any of the nuptials in

May 1994   #533 THE EIGHT-SECOND WEDDING by Anne McAllister
June 1994   #537 THE KIDNAPPED BRIDE by Charlotte Maclay
July 1994   #541 VEGAS VOWS by Linda Randall Wisdom

GTC